DANGE[...]

Rak[...]

Carole M[...] introduces
London's most delectable dukes in her
latest Mills & Boon® Historical mini-series.
But don't be fooled by their charm,
because beneath their lazy smiles they're
deliciously sexy—and highly dangerous!

Read about all the daring exploits
of these dangerous dukes in:

Marcus Wilding: Duke of Pleasure 1
Available as a
Mills & Boon® Historical *Undone!* eBook

Zachary Black: Duke of Debauchery 2

Darian Hunter: Duke of Desire 3

Rufus Drake: Duke of Wickedness 4
Available as a
Mills & Boon® Historical *Undone!* eBook

Griffin Stone: Duke of Decadence 5

And don't miss

Christian Seaton: Duke of Danger 6

Coming September 2015!

Griffin stared down at Bea uncertainly. Either she was the best actress he had ever seen, and she was now attempting to hoodwink him with innocence, or she truly did believe his assurances that he would see she came to no harm while under his protection.

His response to that trust was a totally inappropriate stirring of desire.

Was that so surprising, when she was such a beautiful and appealing young woman? Her eyes that dark and entrancing blue, her lips full and enticing—

What was he thinking?

He had just promised his protection to the woman he had named Bella, only to realise now that he, and the unexpected stirring of his long-denied physical desires, might have become her more immediate danger.

GRIFFIN STONE: DUKE OF DECADENCE

Carole Mortimer

Carole Mortimer was born and lives in the UK. She is married to Peter and they have six sons. She has been writing for Mills & Boon since 1978, and is the author of almost 200 books. She writes for both the Mills & Boon® Historical and Modern™ lines. Carole is a *USA TODAY* bestselling author, and in 2012 was recognised by Queen Elizabeth II for her 'outstanding contribution to literature'.

Visit Carole at carolemortimer.co.uk or on Facebook.

Books by Carole Mortimer

Mills & Boon® Historical Romance and Mills & Boon® Historical *Undone!* eBooks:

Dangerous Dukes

Marcus Wilding: Duke of Pleasure (Undone!)
Zachary Black: Duke of Debauchery
Darian Hunter: Duke of Desire
Rufus Drake: Duke of Wickedness (Undone!)
Griffin Stone: Duke of Decadence

A Season of Secrets

Not Just a Governess
Not Just a Wallflower
Not Just a Seduction (Undone!)

Daring Duchesses

Some Like it Wicked
Some Like to Shock
Some Like it Scandalous (Undone!)

The Copeland Sisters

The Lady Gambles
The Lady Forfeits
The Lady Confesses
A Wickedly Pleasurable Wager (Undone!)

M&B Regency *Castonbury Park* mini-series

The Wicked Lord Montague

Visit the author profile page at millsandboon.co.uk for more titles

To all of you,
for loving the *Dangerous Dukes* as much as I do!

Chapter One

July 1815, Lancashire, England.

'What the—?' Griffin Stone, the tenth Duke of Rotherham, pulled sharply on the reins of his perfectly matched greys as a ghostly white figure ran out of the darkness directly in front of his swiftly travelling phaeton.

Despite his concerted efforts to avoid a collision, the ethereal figure barely missed being stomped on by the high-stepping and deadly hooves, but was not so fortunate when it came to the back offside wheel of the carriage.

Griffin winced as he heard rather than saw that collision, all of his attention centred on bringing the greys to a stop before he was able to jump down from the carriage and run quickly round to the back of the vehicle.

There was only the almost full moon overhead for illumination, but nevertheless Griffin was able to locate where the white figure lay a short distance away.

An unmoving and ghostly shape was lying face down in the dirt.

Two strides of his long legs brought him to the utterly still figure, where he crouched down on his haunches. Griffin could see that the person was female; long dark hair fell across her face and cascaded loosely down the length of her spine, and she was wearing what, to him, looked suspiciously like a voluminous white nightgown, her feet bare.

He glanced about them in confusion; this private way through Shrawley Woods was barely more than a rutted track, and as far as he was aware there were no houses in the immediate vicinity. In fact, Griffin was *very* aware as the surrounding woods and the land for several miles about them formed part of his principal ducal estate.

It made no sense that this woman was

roaming about his woods wearing only her nightgown.

He placed his fingers about her wrist, with the intention of checking for a pulse, only to jerk back as she unexpectedly gave a pained groan the moment his fingers touched her bared flesh. It let him know she was at least still alive, even if the sticky substance he could feel on his fingertips showed she had sustained an injury of some kind.

Griffin took a handkerchief from his pocket and wiped the blood from his hand before reaching out to gently stroke the long dark hair from over her face, revealing it as a deathly pale oval in the moonlight.

'Can you hear me?' His voice was gruff, no doubt from the scare he had received when she'd run out in front of his carriage.

Shrawley Woods was dense, and this rarely used track was barely navigable in full daylight; Griffin had only decided to press on in the darkness towards Stonehurst Park, just a mile away, because he had played in these woods constantly as a child and knew his way blindfolded.

There had been no reason, at eleven o'clock at night, for Griffin to take into account that there would be someone else in these woods. A poacher would certainly have known his way about in a way this barely clothed female obviously did not.

'Can you tell me where you are injured so that I can be sure not to hurt you again?' Griffin prompted, his frown darkening when he received no answer, and was forced to accept that she had once again slipped into unconsciousness.

Griffin made his next decision with the sharp precision for which he had been known in the army. It was late at night, full dark, no one had yet come crashing through the woods in pursuit of this woman, and, whoever she might be, she was obviously in need of urgent medical attention.

Consequently there was only one decision he could make, and that was to place her in the phaeton and continue on with the rest of his journey to Stonehurst Park. Once there they would no longer be in darkness, and he could ascertain her injuries more accurately, after which a doctor could be sent for. Explanations for her state of undress, and her mad flight through the woods, could come later.

Griffin straightened to take off his driving coat and lay it gently across her before scooping her carefully up into his arms.

She weighed no more than a child, her long hair cascading over his arm, her face all pale and dark hollows in the moonlight. He rested her head more comfortably against his shoulder.

She was young and very slender. Too slender. The weight of her long hair seemed almost too much for the slender fragility of her neck to support.

She made no sound as he lifted her up onto the seat of his carriage, nor when he wrapped his coat more securely about her. He took up the reins once again and moved the greys on more slowly than before in an effort not to jolt his injured passenger unnecessarily.

His decision to come to his estate in Lancashire had been forced upon him by circumstances. The open war against Napoleon was now over, thank goodness, but Griffin, and several of his close friends, who also bore the title of Duke and were known collectively as the Dangerous Dukes, all knew, better than most, that there was still a silent, private war to be fought against the defeated emperor and his fanatical followers.

Just a week ago the Dangerous Dukes had helped foil an assassination plot to eliminate their own Prince Regent, along with the other leaders of the alliance. The plan being to ensure Napoleon's victorious return to Paris, while chaos ruled in those other countries.

A Frenchman, André Rousseau, since apprehended and killed by one of the Dangerous Dukes, had previously spent a year in England, secretly persuading men and women who worked in the households of England's politicians and peers to Napoleon's cause. Of which there were many; so many families in England had French relatives.

Many of the perpetrators of that plot had since been either killed or incarcerated, but there remained several who were unaccounted for. It was rumoured that those remaining followed the orders of an as yet unknown leader.

Griffin was on his way to the ducal estates he had not visited for some years, because the Dukes had received word that one of the traitors, Jacob Harker, who might know the identity of this mysterious leader, had been sighted in the vicinity.

It just so happened that three of the Dangerous Dukes had married in recent weeks, and a fourth wed just a week ago, on the very day Griffin had set out for his estate in Lancashire. With all of his friends being so pleasurably occupied, it had been left to him to pursue the rumour of the sighting of Harker.

Running a young woman down in his carriage, in the dark of night, had not been part of Griffin's immediate plans.

She hurt.

Every part of her was in agony and aching as she attempted to move her legs.

A wave of pain that swelled from her toes to the top of her head.

Had she fallen?

Been involved in an accident of some kind?

'Would you care for a drink of water?'

She stilled at the sound of a cultured male voice, hardly daring to breathe as she tried, and failed, to recall if she recognised the owner of it before she attempted to open her eyes.

Panic set in as she realised that he was a stranger to her.

'There is no reason to be alarmed,' Griffin assured her firmly as the young woman in the bed finally opened panicked eyes—eyes that he could now see were the dark blue of midnight, and surrounded by thick lashes that were very black against the pallor of a face that appeared far too thin—and turned to look at him as he sat beside the bed in a chair that was uncomfortably small for his large frame.

She, in comparison, made barely an outline beneath the covers of the bed in his best guest bedchamber at Stonehurst Park, her abundance of long dark hair appearing even blacker against the white satin-and-lace pillows upon which her head lay, her face so incredibly pale.

'I assure you I do not mean you any harm,' he added firmly. He was well aware of the effect his five inches over six feet in height, and his broad and muscled body, had upon ladies as delicate as this one. 'I am sure you will feel better if you drink a little water.'

Griffin turned to the bedside table and poured some into a glass. He placed a hand gently beneath her nape to ease up her head and held the glass to her lips until she had drunk down several sips, aware as he did that those dark blue eyes remained fixed on his every move.

Tears now filled them as her head dropped back onto the pillows. 'I—' She gave a shake of her head, only to wince as even that slight movement obviously caused her pain. She ran her moistened tongue over her lips before speaking again. 'You are very kind.'

Griffin frowned darkly as he turned to place the glass back on the bedside table, hardening his heart against the sight of those tears until he knew more about the circumstances behind this young woman's flight through his woods. His years as an agent for the Crown had left him suspicious of almost everybody.

And women, as he knew only too well, were apt to use tears as their choice of weapon.

'Who are you?'

It was a reasonable question, Griffin supposed, in the circumstances. And yet he could not help but think he should be the one asking that.

When they'd arrived at Stonehurst late last night he had left the care of his carriage and horses to his head groom, before hurriedly taking her into his arms and carrying her up the steps into the house. Once inside he had hurried her up to the bedchambers, much to the open-mouthed surprise of his butler, Pelham.

Rather than send for a doctor straight away Griffin had taken a few moments to assess the condition of the young woman himself. After all, until he knew the reason for her flight through the woods it might be prudent to ask her some questions. Was she in some sort of danger?

Griffin had been grateful for his caution once he had placed his burden carefully down atop the bedcovers and gently folded back the many capes of his topcoat.

As he had thought, the woman was young, possibly eighteen, or at the most twenty, and her heart-shaped face was delicately lovely. She had perfectly arched eyebrows beneath a smooth brow, though the slight hollowness to her cheeks possibly spoke of a deprivation of food. Her nose was small and straight, her mouth a pale pink, the top lip slightly fuller than the bottom, her chin softly curved.

She had been wearing a filthy white cotton nightgown over her slender curves, revealing feet that were both dirty and lacerated beneath its bloodied ankle length. A result, he was sure, that she'd begun her flight shoeless.

There had also already been a sizeable lump and bruising already appearing upon her right temple, no doubt from her collision with his carriage.

But it was her other injuries, injuries that Griffin knew could not possibly have been caused by that collision, which had caused him to draw in a shocked and hissing breath.

The blood he had felt on his fingers earlier came from the raw chafing about both her wrists and ankles. She'd obviously been restrained by tight ropes for some time before her flight through his woods.

There were any number of explanations as to

why she'd been restrained, of course, and not all of them were necessarily sinister.

Though he did not favour the practice himself, he was nevertheless aware that some men liked to secure a woman to the bed—as some women enjoyed being secured!—during love play.

There was also the possibility that this young woman was insane, and had been restrained for her own safety as well as that of others.

The final possibility, and perhaps the most likely, was that she had been restrained against her will.

Until such a time as Griffin established which explanation it was he'd decided that no one in his household, or outside it, was to be allowed to talk to her but himself.

His decision made, Griffin had immediately instructed the hovering Pelham to bring him hot water and towels, and to appropriate a clean nightgown from one of the maids. After all, there had been nothing to stop Griffin making his uninvited guest at least a little more comfortable than she was at present.

Still, he had been deeply shocked, once he

had used his knife to cut the dirty and bloodied nightgown away from her body, to discover many bruises, both old and new, concealed beneath.

There had been no visible marks on her face, apart from the bruise on her temple, but there had been multiple purple and black bruises covering her body, with other, older bruises having faded to yellow. The ridge of her spine had shown through distinctly against that bruised skin as evidence that this woman had not only been repeatedly kicked and or beaten, but that she had also been starved, possibly for some days if not weeks, of more than the food and water necessary to keep her alive.

If that was the case, Griffin was determined to know exactly who was responsible for having exerted such cruelty on this fragile and beautiful young woman, and why.

After assuring she was as comfortable as was possible, Griffin had then gone quickly to his own room to bathe the travel dust from his own body, before changing into clean clothes and returning to spend the night in the chair at her bedside. He'd meant to be at her side when she woke.

If she woke.

She had given several groans of protest as Griffin had bathed the dirt from her wrists, ankles and feet, before applying a soothing salve and bandages, her feet very dirty and badly cut from running outdoors without shoes, and also in need of the application of the healing salve. Otherwise she had remained worryingly quiet and still for the rest of the night.

Griffin, on the other hand, had had plenty of time in which to consider his own actions.

Obviously he could not have left this young woman in the woods, least of all because he was responsible for having rendered her unconscious in the first place. But the uncertainty of who she was and the reasons for her imprisonment and escape meant the ramifications for keeping her here could be far-reaching.

Not that he gave a damn about that; Griffin answered only to the Crown and to God, and he doubted the former had any interest in her, and for the moment—and obviously for some days or weeks previously!—the second seemed to have deserted her.

Consequently Griffin now had the responsibility of her until she woke and was able to tell him the circumstances of her injuries.

Just a few minutes ago Griffin had seen her eyes moving beneath her translucent lids, and her dark lashes flutter against the pallor of her cheeks, as evidence that she was finally regaining consciousness. And her voice, when she had spoken to him at last, had at least answered one of his many questions; her accent was refined rather than of the local brogue, and her manner was also that of a polite young lady.

'I am Griffin Stone, the Duke of Rotherham.' He gave a curt inclination of his head as he answered her question. 'And we are both at Stonehurst Park, my ducal estate in Lancashire.' He frowned as she made no effort to reciprocate. 'And you are?'

And she was…?

Panic once again assailed her as she sought, and failed, to recall her own name. To recall *anything* at all from before she had opened her eyes a few minutes ago and seen the imposing gentleman seated at her bedside in a bed-chamber that was as unfamiliar to her as the man himself.

The Duke of Rotherham.

Even seated he was a frighteningly large man, with fashionably overlong black hair, and impossibly wide shoulders and chest. He was dressed in a perfectly tailored black superfine over a silver waistcoat and white linen, and his thighs and legs were powerfully muscled in grey pantaloons above brown-topped Hessians.

But it was his face, showing that refinement of feature and an expression of aloof disdain, surely brought about only by generations of fine breeding, which held her mesmerised. He had a high intelligent brow with perfectly arched eyebrows over piercingly cold silver-grey eyes. His nose was long and aquiline between high cheekbones, and he'd sculptured unsmiling lips above an arrogantly determined jaw.

He was an intimidating and grimly intense gentleman, with a haughty aloofness that spoke of an innate, even arrogant, confidence. Whereas she...

Her lips felt suddenly numb, and the bedroom began to sway and dip in front of her eyes.

'You must stay awake!' The Duke rose sharply to his feet so that he could take a firm grip of her shoulders, his hold easing slightly only as she gave a low groan of pain. 'I apologise if I caused you discomfort.' He frowned darkly. 'But I really cannot allow you to fall asleep again until I am sure you are in your right mind. So far I have resisted calling the doctor but I fear that may have been unwise.'

'No!' she protested sharply. 'Do not call anyone! Please do not,' she protested brokenly, her fingers now clinging to the sleeves of his jacket as she looked up at him pleadingly.

Griffin frowned his displeasure, not in the least reassured by her responses so far. She seemed incapable of answering the simplest of questions and had now become almost hysterical at his having mentioned sending for the doctor. Had last night's bump to the head caused some sort of trauma to the mind? Or had her mind been affected before?

Griffin knew the English asylums for housing those pitiful creatures were basic at best, and bestial at worst, and tended to attract as warders those members of society least suited to the care of those who were most vulnerable. Admittedly, some of the insane could be violent themselves, but Griffin sincerely doubted that was true in the case of this young woman. She was surely too tiny and slender to be of much danger to others? Unless her jailers had feared self-harm, of course.

Distasteful as that thought might be, Griffin could not deny that it was one explanation for both the bruises on her body, and those marks of restraint.

Except, to his certain knowledge, there was no asylum for the mentally insane situated within fifty miles of Stonehurst Park.

'At least tell me your name,' he said again, more gently this time, for fear of alarming her further.

'I cannot.' The tears now flooded and overflowed, running unchecked down her cheeks and dampening her hair.

Griffin frowned his frustration, with both her tears and her answer.

He was well aware that women cried for many reasons. With pain. In fear. Emotional distress. And to divert and mislead.

And in this instance, it could be being used as a way of not answering his questions at all!

But perhaps he was being unfair and she was just too frightened to answer him truthfully? Fearful of being returned to the place where she had been so cruelly treated?

It would be wrong of him to judge until he knew all the circumstances.

'Are you at least able to tell me why you were running through the Shrawley Woods in the dead of night wearing only your night-clothes?' he urged softly. He was not averse to using his height and size to intimidate a man, but knew only too well how easily those two things together could frighten a vulnerable woman.

'No!' Her eyes had widened in alarm, as if she had no previous knowledge of having run through the woods.

Griffin placed a gentle finger against one of her bandaged wrists. 'Or how you received these injuries?'

She looked blankly down at those bandages. 'I— No,' she repeated emotionally.

Griffin's frustration heightened as he rose restlessly to his feet before crossing the room to where the early morning sun shone brightly through the windows of the bedchamber, the curtains having remained undrawn the night before.

The room faced towards the back of the house, and outside he could see the stirrings of the morning: maids returning to the house with pails of milk, grooms busy in the stables, feeding and exercising the horses, several estate workers already tending to the crops in the far fields.

All normal morning occupations for the efficient running of the estate.

While inside the house all was far from normal.

There was an unknown and abused young woman lying in the bed in Griffin's guest bedchamber, and he knew that his own mood was surly after the long days of travel, and the upset of the collision followed by lack of sleep as he'd sat at her bedside.

Griffin was a man of action.

If something needed to be done, fixed, or solved, then he did, fixed or solved it, and beware anyone who stood in his way.

But he could not do, fix or solve *this* dilemma without this woman's cooperation, and, despite all his efforts to the contrary, she was too fearful at present to dare to confide so much as her name to him.

He knew from personal experience that women often found him overwhelming.

He was certainly not a man that women ever turned to for comfort or understanding. He was too physically large, too overpowering in his demeanour, for any woman to seek him out as their confidant.

No, for their comfort, for those softer emotions such as understanding and empathy, a woman of delicacy looked for a poet, not a warrior.

His wife, although dead these past six years, had been such a woman. Even after weeks of courtship and their betrothal, and despite all Griffin's efforts to reassure her, his stature and size had continued to alarm Felicity.

It had been a fear Griffin had been sure he could allay once they were married. He had been wrong.

'I am not—I do not—I am not being deliberately disobliging or difficult, sir,' she said pleadingly. 'The simple truth is that I cannot tell you my name because—because I do not know it!'

A scowl appeared between Griffin's eyes as he turned sharply round to look across at his unexpected guest, not sure that he had understood her correctly. 'You do not know your own name, or you do not have one?'

Well, of course she must have a name!

Surely everyone had a name?

'I have a name, I am sure, sir.' She spoke huskily. 'It is only—for the moment I am unable to recall it.'

And the shock of realising she did not know her own name, who she was, or how she had come to be here, or the reason for those bandages upon her wrists—indeed, anything that had happened to her before she woke up in this bed a few short minutes ago, to see this aloof and imposing stranger seated beside her— filled her with a cold and terrifying fear.

Chapter Two

The Duke remained still and unmoving as he stood in front of the window, imposing despite having fallen silent after her announcement, those chilling grey eyes now studying her through narrowed lids.

As if he was unsure as to whether or not he should believe her.

And why should he, when it was clear he had no idea as to her identity either, let alone what she had been doing in his woods?

What possible reason could she have had for doing something so shocking? What sort of woman behaved so scandalously?

The possible answer to that seemed all too obvious.

To both her and the Duke?

'You do not believe me.' She made a flat statement of fact rather than asked a question.

'It is certainly not the answer I might have expected,' he finally answered slowly.

'What did you expect?' She struggled to sit up higher against the pillows, once again aware that she had aches and pains over all of her body, rather than just her bandaged wrists. Indeed, she felt as if she had been trampled by several horses and run over by a carriage.

What had Griffin expected? That was a difficult question for him to answer. He had completely ruled out the possibility that she'd sustained her injuries from mutual bed sport; they were too numerous for her ever to have enjoyed or found sexual stimulation from such treatment. Nor did he particularly wish to learn that his suspicions of insanity were true. And the possibility that this young lady might have been restrained against her will, possibly by her own family, was just as abhorrent to him.

But he had never considered for a moment that she would claim to have no memory of her own name, let alone be unable to tell him where or from whom she had received her injuries.

'You do not recall any of the events of last night?'

'What I was doing in the woods? How I came to be here?' She frowned. 'No.'

'The latter I can at least answer.' Griffin strode forcefully across the room until he once again stood at her bedside looking down at her. 'Unfortunately, when you ran so suddenly in front of my carriage, I was unable to avoid a collision. You sustained a bump upon your head and were rendered unconscious,' he acknowledged reluctantly. 'As there are no houses in the immediate area, and no one else was about, I had no choice but to bring you directly here to my own home.'

Then she really *had* been trampled by horses and run over by a carriage.

'As my actions last night gave every appearance of my having known who I was *before* I sustained a bump on the head from the collision with your carriage, is it not logical to assume that it was that collision that is now responsible for my loss of memory?' She eyed him hopefully.

It *was* logical, Griffin acknowledged grudgingly, at the same time as he appreciated her powers of deduction in the face of what must be a very frightening experience for her. He could imagine nothing worse than awakening in a strange bedchamber with no clue to his identity.

Nor did he believe that sort of logic was something a mentally unbalanced woman would be capable of.

If indeed this young woman was being truthful about her memory loss, which Griffin was still not totally convinced about.

The previous night she had been fleeing as if for her very life, would it not be just as logical for her to now *pretend* to have lost her memory, as a way of avoiding the explanations he now asked for? She might fear he'd return her to her abusers.

'Perhaps,' he allowed coolly. 'But that does not explain what you were doing in the woods in your nightclothes.'

'Perhaps I was sleepwalking?'

'You were running, not walking,' Griffin countered dryly. 'And you were bare of foot.'

The smoothness of her brow once again creased into a frown. 'Would that explanation not fit in with my having been walking in my sleep?'

It would, certainly.

If she had not been running as if the devil were at her heels.

If it were not for those horrendous bruises on her body.

And if she did not bear those marks of restraint upon her wrists and ankles.

Bruises and marks of restraint that were going to make it difficult for Griffin to make enquiries about this young woman locally, without alerting the perpetrators of that abuse as to her whereabouts. Something Griffin was definitely reluctant to do until he knew more of the circumstances of her imprisonment and the reason for the abuse. Although there could surely be no excuse for the latter, whatever those circumstances?

He straightened to his fullness of height. 'Perhaps for now we should decide upon a name we may call you by until such time as your memory returns to you?'

'And if it does not return to me?' There was an expression of pained bewilderment in her eyes as she looked up at him.

If her loss of memory was genuine, then the collision with his carriage was not necessarily the cause of it. Griffin had seen many soldiers after battle, mortally wounded and in pain, who had retreated to a safe place inside themselves in order to avoid any more suffering. Admittedly this young woman had not been injured in battle, nor was she mortally injured, but it was nevertheless entirely possible that the things that had been done to her were so horrendous, her mind simply refused to condone or remember them.

Griffin did not pretend to understand the workings of the human mind or emotions, but he could accept that blocking out the memory of who she even was would be one way for this young woman to deal with such painful memories.

For the moment he was willing to give her the benefit of the doubt.

For the moment.

'Bella.'

She blinked her confusion. 'Sorry?'

'Your new name,' Griffin said. 'It means beautiful in Italian.'

'I know what it means.' She *did* know what it meant!

Could that possibly mean that she was of Italian descent? The hair flowing down her shoulders and over her breasts was certainly dark enough. But she did not speak English with any kind of accent that she could detect, and surely her skin was too pale for her to have originated from that sunny country?

And did the fact that the Duke had chosen that name for her mean that he thought her beautiful?

There was a blankness inside her head in answer to those first two questions, her queries seeming to slam up against a wall she could neither pass over nor through. As for the third question—

'I speak French, German and Italian, but that does not make me any of those things.' The Duke was obviously following her train of thought. 'Besides, your first instinct was to speak English.'

'You could be right, of course,' she demurred, all the while wondering whether he did in fact find her beautiful.

What would it be like to be the recipient of the admiration of such a magnificently handsome gentleman as Griffin Stone? Or his affections. His love...

Was it possible she had ever seen such a handsome gentleman as him before today? A gentleman who was so magnificently tall, with shoulders so wide, a chest so muscled, and those lean hips and long and elegant legs? A man whose bearing must command attention wherever he might be?

He was without a doubt a gentleman whom others would know to beware of. A powerful gentleman in stature and standing. A man under whose protection she need never again know fear.

Fear of what?

For a very brief moment she had felt as if she were on the verge of something. Some knowledge. Some *insight* into why she had been running through the woods last night.

And now it was gone.

Slipped from her grasp.

She frowned her consternation as she slowly answered the Duke's observation. 'Or maybe because you spoke to me in English I replied in kind?'

This woman might not be able to answer any of Griffin's questions but he had nevertheless learnt several things about her as the two of them had talked together.

Her voice had remained soft and refined during their conversation.

She was also clearly educated and intelligent.

And, for the moment, despite whatever experiences had reduced her to her present state, she appeared completely undaunted by either his size or his title.

Of course that could be because for now she had much more personal and pressing things to worry about, such as who she was and where she had come from!

Nevertheless, the frankness of her manner and speech towards him was a refreshing change, after so many years of the deference shown to him by other gentlemen of the ton, and the prattling awe of the ladies.

Or the total abhorrence shown to him by his own wife.

He had been but five and twenty when he and Felicity had married. He'd already inherited the title of Duke from his father. Felicity had been seven years younger than himself, and the daughter of an earl. Blonde and petite, she had been as beautiful as an angel, and she had also possessed the other necessary attributes for becoming his duchess: youth, good breeding and refinement.

Felicity might have looked and behaved like an angel but their marriage had surely been made in hell itself.

And Griffin had been thinking of that marriage far too often these past twelve hours, possibly because the delicacy of Bella's appearance, despite their difference in colouring, was so similar to Felicity's. 'We have talked long enough for now, Bella,' he dismissed harshly. 'I will go downstairs now and organise some breakfast for you. You need to eat to regain your strength.'

'Oh, please don't leave! I am not sure I can be alone as yet.' She reached up quickly with both hands and clasped hold of his much larger one, her eyes shimmering a deep blue as she looked up at him in appeal.

Griffin frowned darkly at the fear he could also see in those expressive eyes. A fear not of him—else she would not be clinging to him or appealing to him so emotionally—but certainly of everything and everyone else.

There was a certain irony to be found in the fact that this young woman was showing her implicit trust in him to protect her, when his own wife had so feared the very sight of him that she had eagerly accepted the attentions and warmth of another man.

Damn it, he would not think any more of his marriage, *or* Felicity!

'I am sorry.' Bella hastily released her grasp on the Duke's hand as she saw the scowling displeasure on his face. 'I did not mean to be overly familiar.' She drew her bottom lip between her teeth as she fought back the weakness of tears.

The bed dipped as he sat down beside her, his eyes filled with compassion as he now took one of her hands gently in his. 'It is only natural, in the circumstances, that you should feel frightened and apprehensive.' He spoke gruffly. 'But I assure you that you are perfectly safe here. No one would dare to harm you when you are in my home and under my protection,' he added with that inborn arrogance of his rank.

Bella believed him. Absolutely. Without a single doubt.

Indeed, he was a gentleman whom few would ever dare to doubt, in any way. It was not only that he was so tall and powerfully built, but there was also a hard determination in those chilling grey eyes that spoke of his sincerity of purpose. If he said she would come to no harm while in his home and under his protection, then Bella had no doubt that she would not.

Her shoulders relaxed as she sank back

against the pillows, her hand still resting trustingly in his. 'Thank you.'

Griffin stared down at her uncertainly. Either she was the best actress he had ever seen and she was now attempting to hoodwink him with innocence, or she truly did believe his assurances that he would see she came to no harm while under his protection.

His response to that trust was a totally inappropriate stirring of desire.

Was that so surprising, when he had seen her naked and she was such a beautiful and appealing young woman? Her eyes that dark and entrancing blue, her lips full and enticing, and the soft curve of her tiny breasts—breasts that would surely sit snugly in the palms of his hands?— just visible above the neckline of her—

What was he thinking?

Griffin hastily released her hand as he rose abruptly to his feet to step back and away from the bed. 'I will see that breakfast and a bath are brought up to you directly.' He did not look at her again before turning sharply on his heel and exiting the bedchamber, closing the door firmly behind him before leaning back against it to draw deep breaths into his starved lungs.

He had just promised his protection to the woman he had named Bella, only to now realise that *he*, and the unexpected stirring of his long-denied physical desires, might have become her more immediate danger.

'You are feeling more refreshed, Bella?'

Griffin knew the question was a futile one even as he asked it several hours later, as she stood in the doorway to his study. The walls were lined with the books he enjoyed sitting and reading beside the fireside in the quiet of the evening, a decanter of brandy and glass placed on the table beside him.

At least he *had* intended to enjoy those things the evenings he was here; the advent of his unexpected female guest meant that he might possibly have to spend those evenings entertaining her instead.

He now felt extremely weary following his days of travel and sitting at her bedside all of the previous night.

Bella appeared very pale and dignified as

she remained standing in the doorway, her hair still wet from her bath, scraped back from her face and secured at her crown. She also looked somewhat nondescript in the overlarge pale blue gown borrowed from his housekeeper. It was the best Griffin had been able to do at such short notice, although he had instructed Mrs Harcourt to see about acquiring more suitable clothing for her as soon as was possible.

And if he was not mistaken, Bella had flinched the moment he'd spoken to her.

Unfortunately he knew that flinch too well; Felicity had also recoiled just so whenever he'd spoken to her, so much so that he'd eventually spoken to her as little as was possible between two people who were married to each other and often residing in the same house.

'My feet are still too sore for me to wear the boots provided,' Bella told him quietly, eyes downcast.

Griffin scowled slightly as he looked down at her stockinged feet. She gave all the appearance of a little girl playing dress up in those overly large clothes.

Or the waif and stray that she actually was.

He stood up impatiently from behind his desk. 'They will heal quickly enough,' he dismissed. 'I asked if you are feeling refreshed after your bath,' he questioned curtly, and then instantly cursed himself for that abruptness when Bella took a wary step back, her eyes wide blue pools of apprehension.

The fact that Griffin was accustomed to such a reaction did not make it any more pleasant for him to see it now surface in Bella. But perhaps it was to be expected, now that she was over her initial feelings of disorientation and shock in her surroundings, and had had the chance to fully observe her imposing host?

He leant back against the front of his desk in an effort to at least lessen his height. 'Have you perhaps recalled something of what brought you to Shrawley Woods?'

Bella had been horrified when, after eating a very little of the breakfast brought up for her, she had undressed for her ablutions and seen for the first time the extent of her injuries to her body. She could only feel grateful that she'd seen fit to refuse the attendance of a maid before removing her nightgown as she stared at the naked reflection of her own body in the full-length mirror placed in the corner of the bedchamber.

She was literally covered in bruises. Some of them were obviously new, but others had faded to a sickly yellow and a dirty brown colour, and were possibly a week or so old. As for those strange abrasions, revealed when she removed the bandages from her wrist and her ankles…

How could she have come by such unsightly injuries?

She had staggered back to sit down heavily on the bed as her knees had threatened to buckle beneath her, her horrified gaze still fixed on her naked reflection in the mirror.

She had stared at her bedraggled reflection in utter bewilderment; her long dark hair had been tangled and dull about her shoulders, and there was a livid bruise on her left temple, which the Duke said she had sustained when she and his carriage had collided the night before.

But those other bruises on her body were so unsightly. Ugly!

She had realised then how stupid she had

been to think that he had chosen the name Bella for her because he had thought her beautiful!

Instead it must have been his idea of a jest, a cruel joke at her expense.

'No,' she finally answered stiffly.

Griffin had issued instructions to all of the household staff, through Pelham, that knowledge of the female guest currently residing on the estate was not to be shared outside the house, and that any attempt to do so would result in an instant dismissal. No doubt the servants would do enough gossiping and speculating amongst themselves in that regard, without the necessity to spread the news far and wide!

Griffin, of course, if he was to solve the mystery, had no choice but to also make discreet enquiries in the immediate area for knowledge of a possible missing young lady. And he would have to do this alongside his research into the whereabouts of Harker. But he would carry out both missions with the subtlety he had learnt while gathering information secretly for the Crown. A subtlety that would no doubt surprise many who did not know that the Duke of Rotherham and his closest friends had long been engaged in such activities.

It would have been helpful if the maid who had taken up Bella's breakfast, or any of the footmen who had later taken up her bath, had recognised Bella as belonging to the village or any of the larger households hereabouts. Unfortunately, Pelham had informed him a few minutes ago that that had not been the case.

Confirming that Griffin now had no choice but to try and identify her himself.

In the meantime he had no idea what to do with her!

'Do you play cards?'

She eyed him quizzically as she stepped further into the room. 'I do not believe so, no.'

Griffin watched, mesmerised, as she ran her fingers lingeringly, almost caressingly, along the shelves of books, his imagination taking flight as he wondered how those slender fingers would feel as they caressed the bareness of his shoulders, and down the tautness of his muscled stomach. How soft they would feel as they encircled the heavy weight of his arousal…

'You obviously have a love of books,' he bit out tensely, only to scowl darkly as she immediately snatched her hand back as if burnt before cradling it against her breasts. 'It was an observation, Bella, not a rebuke.' He sighed his irritation, with both his own impatience and her reaction.

'Do not call me by that name!' Fire briefly lit up her eyes. 'Indeed, I believe it to have been exceedingly cruel of you to choose such a name for me!'

Griffin felt at a complete loss in the face of her upset. Three—no, it was now four—of his closest friends were either now married or about to be, and he liked their wives and betrothed well enough. But other than those four ladies the only time Griffin spent in a woman's company nowadays was usually in the bed of one of the mistresses of the demi-monde, and then only for as long as it took to satisfy his physical needs, and with women who did not find his completely proportioned body in the least alarming. Or did not choose to show they did.

His only other knowledge of women was that of his wife, Felicity, and *she* had informed him on more than one occasion that he had no sensitivity, no warmth or understanding in regard to women. Not like the man she had taken as her lover. Her darling Frank, as she had called the other man so affectionately.

Damn Felicity!

If not for Harker, then Griffin would not have chosen to come back here to Stonehurst Park at all. To the place where he and Felicity had spent the first months of their married life together. He had certainly avoided the place for most of the last six years, and being back here now appeared to be bringing back all the bitter and unhappy memories of his marriage.

But if he had not come back to Stonehurst Park last night then what would have become of Bella?

Would she have perhaps stumbled and fallen in the woods in the dark, and perished without anyone being the wiser?

Would the people who had already treated

her so cruelly have recaptured her and returned her to her prison?

For those reasons alone Griffin could not regret now being at Stonehurst Park.

Now if only he could fathom what he had said or done to cause Bella's current upset.

His brow cleared as a thought occurred to him. 'I have already asked my housekeeper to send to the nearest town for more suitable gowns and footwear for you to wear.'

'Suitable gowns and footwear will not make a difference to how I look!' There was still a fire in her eyes as she looked at him. 'How could you be so cruel as to—as to taunt me so, when I am already laid low?'

Griffin gave an exasperated shake of his head. 'I have absolutely no idea what you are talking about.'

'I am talking about this!' She held up the bareness of her bruised arms. 'And this!' She pulled aside the already gaping neckline to reveal her discoloured shoulders. 'And this!'

'Enough! No more, Bella,' Griffin protested as she would have lifted the hem of her gown, hopefully only to show him her abraded calves, but he could not be sure; an overabundance of modesty did not appear to be one of her attributes!

'Bella.' He strode slowly towards her, as if he were approaching a skittish horse rather than a beautiful young woman. 'Bella,' he repeated huskily as he placed a hand gently beneath her chin and raised her face so that he could look directly into her eyes. 'Those bruises are only skin deep. They will all fade with time. And they could never hide the beauty beneath.'

Bella blinked. 'Do you truly mean that or are you just being kind?'

'I believe we have already established that I am cruel rather than kind.'

'I thought—I did not know what to think.' She now looked regretful regarding her previous outburst.

Griffin arched that aristocratic brow. 'I am not a man who is known for his kindness. But neither am I a deceptive one,' he added emphatically.

She gave a shake of her head. 'When I undressed for my bath and saw my reflection in the mirror I could only think that, by giving me such a beautiful name, you must be mocking me for how unsightly I look. I truly believed that you were taunting me.'

'I would never do such a thing to you, Bella,' he assured her softly as he drew her into his arms. 'Never!'

Bella breathed a contented sigh as she lay her head against the firmness of his chest, her arms moving tentatively about the leanness of his waist. He felt so big and strong against her, so solid and sure, like a mountain that would never, could never, be moved.

'Who could have done this to me?' She shuddered as she imagined the beatings she must have received.

Griffin's arms tightened about Bella as he felt her tremble. 'I do not know.' Yet!

For he would learn who was responsible for hurting this young woman. Oh, yes, Griffin would find those responsible for her ill treatment. And when he did—

'Do you think that—?' She buried her head deeper into his chest. 'Could it be that I am a married woman and that perhaps my husband might have done this to me?'

That was a possibility Griffin had not even considered in his earlier deliberations!

Perhaps because she had initially appeared so young to him.

Perhaps because she wore no wedding ring on her left hand.

And perhaps he had not thought of it because he had not wished for her to be a married woman?

But he knew better than most the embarrassment of a cuckolded husband, and Griffin's physical response to Bella was not something he wished, or ever wanted to feel for a woman who was the wife of another man. Not even one who could have treated her so harshly.

Indeed, marriage could be the very worst outcome to Griffin's enquiries regarding Bella; unless otherwise stated in a marriage settlement, English law still allowed that a woman's person, and her property, came under her husband's control upon their marriage. And, if it transpired that Bella was a married woman, then Griffin would be prevented by law from doing anything to protect her from her husband's cruelty, despite his earlier promise to her.

His arms tightened about her. 'Let us hope that does not prove to be the case.'

Bella had sought only comfort when she snuggled into the Duke's arms, seeking an anchor in a world that seemed to her both stormy and precarious.

Since then she had become aware of things other than comfort.

The way Griffin's back felt so firmly muscled and yet so warm beneath her fingers.

The way he smelled: a lemon and sandalwood cologne along with a male earthy fragrance she was sure belonged only to him.

Of what she believed must be his arousal pressing so insistently against the softness of her abdomen as he held her close.

Was it possible that this gentleman, this breathtakingly handsome Duke, this towering man of solidity and strength, was feeling that arousal for *her*?

Griffin became aware of just how perfectly the softness of Bella's curves fitted against his own, much harder body. So perfectly, in fact, that she could not help but be aware of his desire for her.

He pulled back abruptly to place his hands on the tops of her arms as he put her firmly away from him, assuring himself of her balance before he released her completely and stepped back and away from her.

'I have important estate business in need of my urgent attention this morning, so perhaps you might find some way of amusing yourself until luncheon?' He moved to once again sit behind his desk.

He put a necessary distance between the two of them, while the desk now hid the physical evidence of his arousal.

Hell's teeth, he was an experienced man of two and thirty, and far from being a callow youth to be so easily aroused by a woman he had just met. He was also a man who would never again allow himself to fall prey to the vulnerabilities of any woman.

That particular lesson had also been taught to him only too well. His softness of heart had been one of the reasons he had allowed Felicity to charm him into taking her as his wife.

Unbeknown to him, Felicity's father, an earl, had been in serious financial difficulties, and a duke could hardly allow his father-in-law to be carried off to debtors' prison!

Bella felt utterly bewildered by Griffin's sudden rejection of her.

Had she done something wrong to cause him to react in this way?

Been too clinging? Too needy of his comfort?

If she was guilty of those things then surely it had been for good reason?

She felt totally lost in a world that she did not recognise and that did not appear to recognise her. Could she be blamed for feeling that Griffin Stone, the aloof and arrogant Duke of Rotherham, was her only stability in her present state of turmoil?

Blame or otherwise, Bella now discovered that she had resources of pride that this austere Duke's dismissal, the ugliness of her gown, or her otherwise bedraggled and bruised appearance, had not succeeded in diminishing.

Her chin rose. 'I believe I do like books, Your Grace.' Stiltedly she answered his earlier question. 'Perhaps I might borrow one from this library and find somewhere quiet so that I might sit and read it?'

Griffin was feeling a little ashamed of the abruptness of his behaviour now. The more so because he had seen Bella's brief expression of bewilderment at his harsh treatment of her.

Before it was replaced with one of proud determination.

Even wearing that overlarge and unflattering pale blue gown, her feet bare but for her stockings, and with her hair styled so unbecomingly, Bella now bore an expression of haughty disdain worthy of his severe and opinionated grandmother.

The tension eased from his shoulders at that expression, and he settled back against his leather chair. 'If you wish it you might ask Pelham for a blanket, and then go outside and sit beneath one of the trees in the garden. Although I advise that you walk on the safety of the grass until your new footwear arrives,' he added dryly.

Her look of hauteur wavered slightly as she

now eyed him uncertainly. 'I might go out-side?'

'You are not a prisoner here, Bella,' Griffin answered irritably. 'Any restrictions placed on your movements, while you are here, will only be for your own safety and never as a way of confining you,' he added with a frown.

The slenderness of her throat moved as she swallowed before answering. 'And what if we were never to discover who I really am?'

Then he would keep her.

And buy her dozens of pretty gowns of a fit and colour that flattered her, and the slippers to match. Then he would feed her until she burst out of those gowns and needed new ones, her cheeks rosy with—

Griffin's mouth firmed as he brought an abrupt halt to the unsuitability of his thoughts. He could not *keep* Bella, even if she were fool-ish enough to want to stay with him. She was not a dog or a horse, and a duke did not *keep* a young woman, unless she was his mistress, and Bella was far too young and beautiful to be interested in such a relationship with a gen-tleman so much older than herself.

Nor did Griffin have any interest in taking a mistress. A few hours of enjoyment here and there with the ladies of the demi-monde was one thing, the setting up of a mistress something else entirely.

Even if his physical response to Bella was undeniable.

Chapter Three

'People do not just disappear, Bella,' he now bit out grimly. 'Someone, somewhere, knows exactly who you are.'

Bella supposed that had to be true; after all, she could not have just suddenly appeared in the world as if by magic.

Oh, but it had been so wonderful, just for those few brief seconds, to imagine being allowed to stay here. To remain at Stonehurst Park for ever, with this proud and arrogant Duke, who she was sure had a kind heart, despite the impression he might wish to give to the contrary. After all, he had not hesitated to care for her, despite the circumstances under which he had found her.

She felt sure that a less kind man would have

handed her over to the local magistrate by now, in fear she might be a criminal of some sort, rather than allowing her to remain in his household. For if it transpired she was a thief, then he could not be sure she might not steal all the family silver before escaping into the night. And she might do so much more if she were more than a thief…

No, despite his haughty aloofness, his moments of harshness, and that air of proud and ducal disdain, Bella could not believe Griffin to be anything other than a kind man.

Besides which, she had not imagined the physical evidence of his desire for her a few minutes ago.

She looked at him shyly from beneath her lashes. 'Then I can only hope, whoever they might be, that they do not find me *too* quickly.'

Exactly what did she mean by *that*? Griffin wondered darkly.

He had come to Stonehurst Park for the sole purpose of finding Harker; the last thing he needed was the distraction of a mysterious woman he found far too physically disturbing for his own comfort!

A conclusion he was perhaps a little late in arriving at, when that young woman currently stood before him, barefoot, and a guest in his home…

The mysteries of her circumstances aside, Bella was something of an unusual young woman. The slight redness to her eyes was testament to the fact that she had been recently crying, which he was sure any woman would have done given her current situation. But most women would also have been having a fit of the vapours at the precariousness, the danger, of their present dilemma. Bella appeared calm, almost accepting.

As evidence that she did not, as he suspected, suffer from amnesia at all?

He looked at her coldly from between narrowed lids. 'The sooner the better as far as I am concerned.'

Bella frowned at the coldness of his tone. Just when she had concluded that Stone must be a kind man he did or said something to force her to decide the opposite. As if in self-defence?

She turned away to look at the shelves of

books so that he should not see the hurt in her eyes, glad when the heaviness of her heart lightened somewhat just at the sight of those books. As proof that she did indeed like to read?

She took a novel down from the shelf. 'I believe I shall read *Sense and Sensibility*. I have read it before, but it has long been a favourite of—' Bella broke off, her expression one of open-mouthed disbelief as she realised what she had just done. 'Oh, my! Did you hear what I said?' she prompted eagerly.

The Duke's mouth twisted without humour. 'I believe that happens sometimes with people who have lost their memory. They recall certain likes and dislikes, such as a foodstuff, or a book they have read, but not specifics about themselves.'

'Oh.' Bella's face dropped in disappointment. 'I had thought for a moment that I might be recovering my memory, and so relieving you of my presence quite soon, after all.'

Griffin knew that he deserved her sharpness, after speaking to her so abruptly and dampening her enthusiasm so thoroughly just now. He had been exceedingly rude to her.

But what was he to do when he was so aware of every curve of her body, even in that ghastly gown? When she had felt so soft and yielding in his arms just minutes ago? When the clean womanly smell of her, after the strong perfume and painted ladies of the demi-monde, was stimulation enough? When just the sight of her stockinged feet peeping out from beneath her gown sent his desire for her soaring?

Why, just minutes ago he had been thinking of *keeping* her!

Damn it, he could not, he *would* not, allow himself to become in any way attached to this young woman, other than as a surrogate avuncular figure who offered her aid in her distress. Chances were Bella would be gone from here very soon, possibly even later today or tomorrow, if his enquiries today should prove fruitful.

He deliberately turned his attention to the papers on his desk. 'Do not go too far from the house,' he instructed distractedly. 'We have no idea as yet who is friend or foe.' He glanced up seconds later when Bella had made no effort to leave or acknowledge what he'd said.

'What?' He frowned darkly.

She eyed him quizzically. 'I was wondering if that follows you around constantly.'

Griffin's irritation deepened at her enigmatic comment. 'If what follows me around?' He had owned a hound as a child but never as a man...

'That black thundercloud hanging over your head.'

Griffin stared at her for several long seconds as if he had indeed been thunderstruck. He had also, he realised dazedly, been rendered completely speechless.

Did he have a thundercloud hanging over his head?

Quite possibly.

There had been little in his past, or of late, for him to smile about. Nor, he would have thought, too much to cause amusement to this young woman either, but Bella now gave him a mischievous smile.

'If that should be the case, I sincerely hope it does not rain on you too often.'

Impudent minx!

Despite his best efforts he could not prevent the smile of amusement from curving his lips, followed by a sharp bark of outraged laughter as Bella continued to look at him with that feigned innocence in her candid blue eyes.

Bella's breath caught in her throat as Griffin began to chuckle, finding herself fascinated by the transformation that laughter made to the usual austereness of his face. Laughter lines had appeared beside now warm grey eyes, two grooves indenting the rigidness of his cheeks, his sculptured lips curling back to reveal very white and even teeth.

He was, quite simply, the most devastatingly handsome gentleman she had ever seen!

Perhaps.

For how could she say that with any certainty, when she did not so much as know her own name?

She gave a shiver as the full weight of that realisation once again crashed down on her. What if she *should* turn out to be a thief, or something worse, and last night she had been fleeing from imprisonment for her crimes?

She did not *feel* like a criminal. Had not felt any desire earlier, as she'd made her way through this grand house to the Duke's study, to steal any of the valuables, the silver, or the paintings so in abundance in every room and hallway she passed by or through. Nor did she feel any inclination to cause anyone physical harm—except perhaps to crash the occasional vase over the Duke's head, when he became so annoyingly cold and dismissive.

Except there weren't any vases in this room, Bella realised as she looked curiously about the study. Nor had she seen any flowers in the cavernous hallway to brighten up the entrance to the house.

That was what she would do!

When she asked Pelham for a blanket to sit on outside, she would also enquire about something with which to cut some of the flowers, growing so abundantly in the garden she could see outside the windows, and she'd ask for a basket to put them in.

Just because she had no idea who she was, or what she was doing here, was no reason for her not to attempt in some small way to repay the Duke's kindness in allowing her to remain in his home. And this beautiful house would look so much more welcoming with several vases of flowers placed—

'What are you plotting now?' Griffin's laughter had faded as suddenly as it had appeared, and he now eyed Bella warily as he saw the light of determination that had appeared so suddenly in her eyes.

She frowned as her attention snapped back to him. 'Why do you treat me with so much suspicion?' She gave a shake of her head. 'I know that the circumstances of my being here are unusual, to say the least, but that is hardly my fault, or a reason for you to now accuse me of plotting anything.'

Griffin heaved a weary sigh, very aware that he was projecting his wariness and suspicions onto Bella, emotions so familiar to him because of Felicity's duplicity. Which was hardly fair or reasonable of him.

He nodded abruptly. 'I apologise. Perhaps I am just tired after my disturbed night's sleep,' he excused ruefully. 'Please do go and enjoy reading your book out in the garden, and try to forget that I am such a bad-tempered bore.'

Griffin was far from a bad-tempered bore to her, Bella acknowledged wistfully. No, the Duke of Rotherham was more of an enigma to her than a bad-tempered bore. As he surely would be to most people.

So tall and immensely powerful of build, he occasionally demonstrated a gentleness to her that totally belied that physical impression of force and power. Only for him to then address or treat her with a curtness meant, she was sure, to once again place her at arm's length.

As if he was annoyed with himself, for having revealed even that amount of gentleness.

As if he were in fear of it.

Or of her?

Bella gave a snort at the ridiculousness of that suggestion as she glanced at him, and saw he was already engrossed in the papers on his desk. He did not even seem to notice her going as she took her book and left the study to walk despondently out into the garden.

No, the differences in their stature and social standing—whatever her own might be, though it surely could in no way match a duke's illustrious position in society?—must surely ensure that Bella posed absolutely no threat to Griffin. In any way.

In all probability, the Duke was merely annoyed with being forced to continue keeping the nuisance of her, and the mystery of her, here in his home.

She had not *asked* to be here, or to foist the puzzle of who she was upon him.

Nevertheless, that was exactly what had happened.

But where else could she go, and *how* could she go, when she had no friends or money with which to do so?

Like a moth to a flame Griffin found himself getting restlessly back onto his feet and wandering over to the window within minutes of Bella leaving the library, the papers on his desk holding no interest for him whatsoever.

At least, none that could compete with his curiosity in regard to the mystery that was Bella.

She had already spread a blanket on the

grass and was now sitting beneath the old oak tree he could see from the window, the book open in her hand, the darkness of her still-damp hair loose again about her shoulders, now drying in the dappled sunlight filtering through the lush branches above her.

What *was* Griffin going to do with her, if his enquiries as to her identity should prove unsatisfactory?

She could not remain here indefinitely; if it turned out that she came from a family in society, as he suspected she might, then her reputation would be blackened for ever if anyone should realise she had stayed in his home without the benefit of a chaperone or close relative.

Inviting *his* only close relative to come to Stonehurst Park and act as that chaperone was totally unacceptable to Griffin; he and his maternal grandmother were far too much alike in temperament to ever be able to live under the same roof together, even for a brief period of time.

Perhaps he should send word to Lord Aubrey Maystone in London? He worked at the Foreign Office, and was the man to whom Griffin reported directly in his ongoing work for the Crown.

The puzzle of Bella was not a subject for the Foreign Office, of course. Nor was it cause for concern regarding the Crown. But Maystone had many contacts and the means of garnering information that were not available to Griffin. Most especially so here in the wilds of Lancashire.

Except…

Maystone had been put in the position of shooting one of the conspirators himself the previous month, and after that he'd become even fiercer in regard to the capture of the remaining conspirators. If Griffin were to tell the older man about Bella, he could not guarantee that Maystone would not instruct that Bella must be brought to London immediately for questioning, for fear she too was involved in that assassination plot in some way.

He might never see Bella again—

His gaze sharpened as he saw that while he had been lost so deep in thought, Bella had risen to her feet and left the shade of the oak tree to walk across the garden. She now stood in conversation with the gardener who had been working on one of the many flower beds.

This was not the elderly Hughes, who had been head gardener here even in Griffin's father's time, but a much younger man Griffin did not recognise. A handsome, golden-haired young man, in his early twenties, who was obviously enjoying looking at Bella as that dark hair hung loosely about her shoulders, as much if not more than the conversation.

Just as Bella appeared perfectly relaxed and smiling as the two of them chatted together.

Griffin did not give himself time to think as he turned to stride forcefully out of his study to walk down the hallway, leaving the house by the side door usually only reserved for the servants, before crossing the perfectly manicured lawn towards the still-conversing couple.

A handsome young man and beautiful woman so engrossed in each other they did not yet seem aware of his presence.

Bella broke off her conversation and her eyes widened in alarm the moment she spied the tall and fiercely imposing Duke storming across the grass towards her, his face as dark as that thundercloud he carried around above his head.

Her heart immediately started to pound in her chest, and the palms of her hands felt damp. What on earth could have happened to cause such a reaction in him?

'Your Grace?' She looked up at him uncertainly as he reached her side.

'Who are you?'

The glowering Duke ignored her, his countenance becoming even more frightening as he instead looked at the young gardener with cold and frosty eyes.

'Sutton, Your Grace. Arthur Sutton.' The young man touched a respectful hand to his forelock, his face becoming flushed under the older man's cold stare.

'You may go, Sutton.' Griffin nodded an abrupt dismissal. 'And I would appreciate it if you would take yourself off to work elsewhere on the estate for the rest of the day,' he added harshly, causing the bewildered young man to turn away and quickly collect up his tools ready for departing.

Bella felt equally bewildered by the harshness of Griffin's tone and behaviour. It was almost as if he suspected her and the gardener of some wrongdoing, of some mischief, when all they had been doing was—

'Oh!' She gasped after glancing towards the house to see that the library window overlooked this garden, and realised *exactly* what Griffin had suspected her and the handsome gardener of doing.

Bella made sure that the young gardener had walked far enough away out of earshot, before she glared up into the harshly drawn face looking down at her so condescendingly. 'How could you?'

The Duke quirked that infuriatingly superior eyebrow. 'How could I what?'

'You know exactly what I am talking about.' Bella sighed her impatience. 'How can you have been so disgusting as to have thought— to suggest, that I—that we—?' She was too angry to say any more as she instead turned sharply on her stockinged heels to run back towards the house.

Hateful man.

Hateful, suspicious, disgusting man!

Griffin stood unmoving for several seconds after Bella had departed so abruptly, totally taken aback by her reaction. To the anger she had made no effort to hide from him as she'd spoken to him so accusingly.

Why was she angry with him, when *she* was the one who had been—?

The one who had been what?

Exactly what had Griffin actually seen from the library window?

The beautiful Bella in her overlarge gown, with her gloriously black hair loose and curling down the length of her spine, in conversation with one of his under-gardeners.

A young and handsome under-gardener, accepted, but Bella had not been standing scandalously close to Sutton, nor had she been behaving in a flirtatious manner towards him. Admittedly she had been smiling as she chatted so easily with the younger man, but even that was not reason enough for Griffin to have made the assumption he had.

Could it be that he had been *jealous* of her easy conversation and laughter with the younger man?

Was it possible that he thought, because of the unusual circumstances of Bella being here with him at all, that her smiles and laughter belonged only to him?

That *she* now somehow belonged to him?

'Bella?'

She stiffened and ceased her crying, but made no effort to lift her head from the pillow into which it was currently buried as she lay face down on the bed.

She made no verbal acknowledgement of Griffin's presence in her bedchamber at all. Correction, *his* bedchamber. As all of this magnificent house, and the extensive estate surrounding it, also belonged to him.

And she, having absolutely no knowledge of her past or even her name, was currently totally beholden to him.

But that did not mean Griffin Stone had the right to treat her with such suspicion. That he could virtually accuse her of flirting with Arthur Sutton. Or worse...

The under-gardener had been *nice*. A young man who had not been in the least familiar in his manner towards her, but rather accepted her as a guest of the Duke, and had treated her accordingly.

Not that she could expect Griffin to believe that when his mind was so obviously in the gutter.

What had she done to deserve such suspicion from him?

Admittedly, the circumstances of their meeting had been unusual to say the least, but surely there had to be an explanation for that?

Even if she had no idea as yet what that explanation was…

Besides which, she was so obviously battered and bruised, it was ludicrous to imagine that any man might find her attractive in her present state.

Although, there was no denying that Griffin himself had physically reacted to her close proximity earlier.

Perhaps it was just that he was a little odd, if he was attracted to a woman who was covered in bruises!

Which was a little worrying, now that Bella considered the possibility fully.

The Duke did not look like a gentleman who enjoyed inflicting pain, but that was no reason to suppose—

'I apologise, Bella.'

The bed dipped beside her as the Duke, obviously tired of waiting for her response to his initial overture, now sat down on the side of the bed.

'Bella?'

Her body went rigid as he placed a hand lightly against her spine. 'We both know that is not my name.' Her voice was muffled as she spoke into the pillow.

'I thought we had agreed that it would do for now?' he cajoled huskily.

Until they discovered what her name really was, Bella easily picked up on his unspoken comment.

If they ever discovered what her name really was, she added inwardly.

Which was part of the reason she had been so upset when she'd returned to the house just now.

Oh, there was no doubting this aloof and arrogant Duke had behaved appallingly out in the garden just now; he had spoken with unwarranted terseness to Arthur Sutton, and had certainly been disrespectful to her. His implied accusations regarding the two of them had been insulting, to say the least.

Bella's previous treatment, as well as her present precarious situation, meant that her tears were all too ready to fall at the slightest provocation…

Griffin Stone's behaviour in the garden had not been slight, but extreme.

Bella slipped out from beneath his hand before rolling over to face him, hardening her heart as she saw the way he looked down at her in apology. She had been enjoying her time out in the garden, and he had now spoilt that for her.

For those brief moments she had spoken with Arthur Sutton she had felt *normal*, and not at all like the bedraggled and beaten woman the Duke had found in the woods the previous night.

Her chin rose challengingly. 'Your behaviour in the garden—the cold way you spoke to Arthur Sutton, as well as to me—was unforgivably condescending.'

Griffin only just managed to hold back his smile as Bella administered the rebuke so primly. To smile now would be a mistake on his part, when Bella was so obviously not in the mood to appreciate the humour.

'And wholly undeserved,' she added crossly as some of that primness deserted her to be replaced by indignation. 'You may well be overlord here, Your Grace, but that does not permit you to make assumptions about other people. Assumptions, I might add, that in this case were wholly unfounded.'

Oh, yes, this young woman was certainly educated and from a titled or wealthy family, Griffin acknowledged ruefully; that set-down had been worthy of any of the grand ladies of the ton!

Did Bella even realise that? he wondered.

Possibly not, when she had no knowledge of anything before her arrival here last night.

Appeared to have no knowledge, he again reminded himself.

There was still that last lingering doubt in

Griffin's mind regarding her claim of amnesia. Added to, no doubt, by his having just observed her in conversation with one of his under-gardeners.

What if she had been passing information on to Arthur Sutton? If her arrival here in his home had been premeditated?

Shortly before the assassination plot against the Prince Regent had been foiled several of Maystone's agents had been compromised. Griffin had been one of them.

There was always the possibility that Bella had been deliberately planted in his home, of course. That she was here to gather information from him as to how deeply their circle had been penetrated.

And he was becoming as paranoid as Maystone!

Nor was it an explanation that made sense, when Griffin considered those marks of restraint upon Bella's wrists and ankles.

Alternatively perhaps she had been talking to Arthur Sutton in an effort to find some way in which she might leave Stonehurst Park without his knowledge.

And what if she had?

If Bella were to disappear as suddenly as she had arrived, then surely it would be a positive thing, as far as Griffin was concerned, rather than a negative one?

He would not have to give her a second thought this afternoon, for example, when he rode out to pay calls on his closest neighbours, in his search for information on Harker.

Nor would there be need to write to Aubrey Maystone in London to ask for his assistance, and possibly at the same time alert the other Dangerous Dukes to his present dilemma by doing so; in their work as agents for the Crown they all of them had or still reported to Maystone. Ordinarily Maystone would not discuss any individual agent's business with a third party, but the older man was well aware of the close friendship between the Dangerous Dukes, and might feel obliged to mention his concerns to them.

The last thing Griffin wanted was for one or all of his closest friends to decide to come to Stonehurst Park to offer him their assistance.

Lord knew he had felt displeased, even proprietorial, merely watching Arthur Sutton in conversation with Bella, so how would he feel if any of his much more attractive friends were to come here and proceed to exert their considerable charms on her?

Admittedly only Christian Seaton, the Duke of Sutherland, still remained single out of those five friends, but Christian possessed a lethal charm as well as handsome looks. Women had been known to swoon when confronted by them.

'What were you and Sutton talking about, Bella?' Griffin demanded harshly, determined to remain in control of his wandering thoughts.

Bella frowned as she pushed herself up against the pillows; she felt at far too much of a disadvantage with Griffin looming over her in that way. 'Should you not offer me an apology before making demands for explanations?'

The Duke's jaw tightened. 'I apologised a few minutes ago. An apology you chose not to acknowledge.'

'Because it was far too ambiguous,' she told him impatiently. 'As it did not state what it was you were apologising for.'

The Duke closed his eyes briefly, as if just looking at her caused him exasperation. As no doubt it did. He had not asked to have her company foisted upon him, and whatever his own plans had been for this morning he had surely had to abandon them. Also because of her.

His eyes were an icy grey when he raised his lids to look at her. 'It was not my intention to upset you.'

Bella raised dark brows. 'Then what was your intention?'

Griffin wondered if counting to ten—a hundred!—might help in keeping him calm in the face of Bella's determination to demand an explanation from him. 'I was concerned that Sutton might have been bothering you.'

A frown appeared between her eyes. 'How could that be, when I was obviously the one who had walked over to where he was working, rather than him approaching me?'

Griffin's mouth thinned as he acknowledged that fact. 'And I ask again, what were the two of you talking about?'

'The weather, perhaps?' she snapped, her irritation obvious.

'I warn you not to try my patience any further today, Bella,' Griffin rasped coldly.

Bella *was* deliberately provoking Griffin, and she knew she was. But with good reason, she believed.

She might not recall anything about herself, but this proud and arrogant Duke did not know anything about her either, and she resented—deeply—that, having seen her in conversation with Arthur Sutton, he had made certain assumptions regarding her nature.

She sat up fully to wrap her arms about her bent knees. 'If you must know, I was asking Arthur for a trug and something to cut the flowers to put in it.'

'Why?' Heavy lids now masked the expression in Griffin's eyes, but his increased tension was palpable, nonetheless.

'This is such a beautiful house and the addition of several vases of flowers would only enhance—'

'No.'

Bella blinked her uncertainty at the harshness of his tone. 'No?'

'No.' He stood up abruptly, towering over

her, his hands linked behind his back as he once again looked down the length of his aristocratic nose at her. 'I do not permit vases of flowers in any of my homes.'

'Why on earth not?' She gave a puzzled shake of her head. 'Everyone likes flowers.'

'I do not,' he bit out succinctly, a nerve pulsing in his tightly clenched jaw.

He was currently at his most imposing, his most chilling, Bella acknowledged. She had no idea why the mention of a vase of flowers should have caused such a reaction in him. 'You are allergic, perhaps?'

His laugh was bitterly dismissive. 'Not in the least. I am merely assured that the beauty of flowers is completely wasted on a man such as me.'

'Assured by whom?' Bella frowned her deepening confusion.

His eyes glittered coldly. 'By my wife!'

His *wife*?

Griffin, the Duke of Rotherham, the man who had saved her from perishing alone and lost in the woods, the man she felt so drawn to, the same man who had physically reacted to her close proximity this morning, had a *wife*?

Chapter Four

Why was Bella so surprised to learn that the Duke of Rotherham had a wife?

He was a very handsome gentleman, and wealthy too, judging by the meticulous condition of this beautiful estate. *Of course* such a man would have a wife. A beautiful and accomplished duchess, to complement his own chiselled good looks and ducal haughtiness. And, no doubt, to provide him with the necessary heirs.

Was it possible he already had several of those children in his nursery?

Bella swallowed before speaking again. 'I did not know…I had no idea…I had assumed—' She had *assumed* that Griffin was unmarried. That the way she felt so inexplicably drawn towards him was acceptable, even as she acknowledged it was altogether impossible that that interest would ever be felt in return for the vagabond she currently was. 'Why have I not yet been introduced to your wife?'

A nerve pulsed in his tightly clenched cheek. 'Obviously because she is not here.'

Bella felt totally bewildered by the coldness of his tone.

'Then where is she?'

His eyes were now glacial. 'She has been buried in the family crypt in the village churchyard these past six years.'

Oh, dear Lord!

Why had she continued to question and pry? Why could she not have just left the subject alone, when she could see that it was causing Griffin such terrible discomfort? The stiffness of his body, the tightness of his jaw, and the over-bright glitter of his eyes were all proof of that.

But no, because she was irritated with him over his earlier behaviour, those ridiculous assumptions he had made concerning her conversation with Arthur Sutton, she had continued to push and to pry into something that was surely none of her business. Into a subject that obviously caused this proud and haughty man immense pain.

'Do you have children, too?'

His mouth tightened. 'No.'

'How did she die?' Bella knew she really should not ask any more questions, but the look on Griffin's face indicated that if she did not ask them now she might never be given another opportunity. And she wanted to *know*.

Besides which, Griffin could only be aged in his early thirties now, and he said his wife had been dead for six years, so surely that wife could not have been any older than her early to mid-twenties when she died?

'She drowned,' he bit out harshly.

'How?' Bella gasped.

'I will not discuss this subject with you any further, Bella!'

Bella knew she really had pushed the subject as far as Griffin would allow, as he turned away to look out of the bedroom window.

She hesitated only briefly, her gaze fixed on the rigid set of his shoulders and unyielding back as she swung her legs to the floor, before rising quickly to her feet to cross over to where the Duke stood. 'Now it is my turn to apologise.' Her voice was huskily soft as she stood behind him. 'I should not have continued to ask questions about something that so obviously distresses you.'

He made no response, indeed he gave no indication he had even heard her.

Bella waited for several long seconds before lifting her arms up tentatively and sliding them gently about his waist, hearing him draw in a hissing breath as she did so. She could feel the way that his body became even more rigid beneath her hands as she rested them on his abdomen.

Realising her mistake, she started to draw away.

'No!' Griffin's hands moved up to hold those slender arms about his waist. 'Stay exactly where you are,' he ordered as his body relaxed against Bella's warmth and the soft press of her breasts against his back.

It had been so long since any woman had voluntarily offered him the comfort of her arms other than for that brief prelude occasionally offered before the sexual act began.

Griffin's eyes closed as he now savoured the sensation of just being held. Of having no expectations asked of him, other than to stand here and accept those slender arms about his waist. At the same time as Bella's softness continued to warm him through his clothing.

Griffin had not realised until now just how much he had missed having a woman's undemanding and tenderness of feeling. He had not allowed himself to feel hunger for those things that he knew could never be his.

He had to marvel at Bella, giving that tenderness and warmth so freely, when circumstances surely dictated she was the one in need of that comfort.

For the moment Griffin did not want to think about those circumstances, to give thought to the fact he knew nothing about this young woman. Why should he, when he had known even less about the women in whose bodies he had taken his pleasure these past six years? No, for now he intended to simply *enjoy* the moment.

Bella had not moved since Griffin had instructed her not to. But she still couldn't stop thinking about the wife he'd lost so tragically.

Had Griffin been very much in love with her?

Had their marriage been a happy one?

Had Griffin been nursing a broken heart since losing his wife?

Could that broken heart be the reason he had never remarried?

'Your thoughts are so loud, Bella, I can almost hear them,' Griffin chided dryly.

'Can you?' she breathed shallowly, sincerely hoping that was not the case. Griffin seemed such a private man, so closed off within himself, that she was sure he would not appreciate learning of the many questions about him still raging inside her head.

'Oh, yes,' he murmured as he slowly turned in her arms.

Bella's breath caught in her throat as she found herself so suddenly facing him. It had been so much easier to hold Griffin when she was not looking up into his mesmerising and handsome face.

When she could still breathe.

When her thoughts had not suddenly turned to mush.

When he could not see how her body was betraying her responses to him. Her face felt flushed, eyes fever-bright, and the tips of her breasts had become swollen and sensitive beneath the material of her overlarge gown. She also felt an unfamiliar sensation low down between her thighs.

Griffin's large hands moved up to cup her cheeks as he tilted her face up to his, looking down searchingly. 'Are you a witch?' he murmured gruffly.

Bella could not look away from the compelling heat in those silver eyes. 'I do not think so.'

He gave a slow shake of his head. 'I think you must be.'

'Why must I?'

His eyes darkened, his expression grim. 'Because you have made me want you!'

Her heart leapt in her chest at the fierceness with which he delivered the admission.

There was such an unmistakeable underlying anger in Griffin's voice, telling her that he resented those feelings.

Because he still loved his dead wife, and the desire he now felt for Bella was a betrayal to those feelings?

Or was his anger with himself rather than her, for feeling that desire for someone he did not know or completely trust?

He gave a humourless laugh. 'You can have no idea how much I envy you, Bella!'

She blinked at the strangeness of the comment. 'Why on earth would you envy me?' At the moment she had nothing. No past.

No future. No *name*. Even the dress she was wearing belonged to another woman.

Griffin's hands tightened against her cheeks. 'Because your lack of knowledge about your past means you have no memory of pain or loss, either. Or the mistakes you might have made,' he rasped harshly. 'Because the blank of that past allows you to start afresh. To decide what that past might have been, and to make the future your own.'

That was one way of looking at this situation, Bella supposed.

Except she would much rather know her past. Whatever that past might be.

To not know who or what she was gave her the constant feeling of walking along the edge of a precipice, when one misguided step or action would hurtle her over the edge of that precipice to her certain death.

She moistened her lips with the tip of her tongue. A movement Griffin followed hungrily, causing Bella's heart to falter in her chest as she found herself suddenly unable to speak.

'You *are* a witch,' Griffin groaned throatily, no longer able to resist the lure of wanting to feel those lush and rosy-coloured lips beneath his own. He lowered his head towards hers.

Her gently parted lips felt as soft as rose petals beneath his, as he held back his hunger to plunder and claim but instead kissed her with restrained gentleness, her taste as sweet as the nectar between those petals. A nectar Griffin wanted to lap up greedily with his tongue.

Dear Lord!

Griffin groaned low in his throat, hungrily deepening the kiss as he felt the tentative sweep of Bella's tongue against his own like hot enveloping silk, her arms now clinging tightly about his waist as she pressed the soft length of her body eagerly against his much harder one. So eager, so trusting.

Damn it, he had made a promise to Bella to protect her while she remained in his household. And she had left him in no doubt that she now trusted him to ensure her safety. Even from himself.

It took every effort of willpower on his part, but he finally managed to gather the strength to wrench his mouth from hers, breathing heavily as he put her firmly away from him before releasing her.

He hardened his heart against the look of pained rejection in Bella's reproachful gaze. If he weakened, even for a moment, he would give in to the temptation to take her back into his arms. And he knew that this time he would be unable to stop kissing her, touching her, caressing her, and it would end with him craving more than she was ready to give.

'It is past time I returned to my study,' he barked before turning sharply to cross the room to the door.

Bella reached out a hand to grasp the back of the chair nearest to her, barely able to stand on her own two feet. The onslaught of emotions she had known in Griffin's arms had left her feeling light-headed.

'I will be going out for some time after luncheon, paying calls to some of my neighbours,' the Duke—for that was surely who Griffin now was; that aloof and disdainful Duke whom she had met this morning!—informed her distantly.

'Do you wish me to accompany you?' Bella had no idea how she felt about leaving the safety of this estate. Fear, perhaps, at going out into a world she did not know?

As much as she felt a nervousness at the thought of Griffin being nowhere nearby for her to call to if she should need him?

'I believe, for the moment, you should remain here, out of sight,' he dismissed coldly, his back still turned towards her as he paused with his hand on the door handle of the bedchamber. 'You may pick some flowers from the garden, and bring them into the house, if you wish.'

There was no doubt in Bella's mind that he

made the concession as an apology. Whether that apology was for his mistaken accusations over Arthur Sutton, or for kissing her just now, she had no idea.

Either way, Bella did not need to be humoured as if she were a child!

She had been a willing participant in their kisses just now, and she had revelled in the experience, in the rush of emotions she had felt at being held so tightly in Griffin's arms: pleasure, arousal, heat.

His rejection just minutes later had been as if a shower of cold water had been thrown over her.

She gathered herself up to her full height as she stepped away from the chair. 'I do not wish, thank you.'

Griffin gave a wince as he heard the hurt beneath Bella's haughtiness of tone.

Because he had called a halt to their kisses?

Because she had enjoyed them as much as he had?

But what other choice did he have but to stop? She was a young woman staying as a guest in his household. A vulnerable young woman he had offered his protection to for as long as she had need of it. She said she trusted him.

Yet surely he had just violated that trust?

He would not be accused of violating her too!

Griffin gave a terse inclination of his head. 'Do as you please,' he dismissed coolly even as he wrenched open the door to the bedchamber and made good his escape.

Bella blinked back the tears of self-pity that now blurred her vision. She would not allow herself to cry again.

She refused to cry simply because Griffin so obviously regretted kissing her.

But what a kiss!

Delivered with a depth of feeling, a passion, that had shaken her to the core.

Had it also shaken Griffin?

He had been so cold when he'd pulled away from her so suddenly. Very much the Duke of Rotherham.

He was tired of her, tired of the burden she'd become.

Perhaps it would be best for both of them if she were to leave here.

To leave Griffin.

Griffin's mood was one of deep impatience by the time he rode through the Shrawley Woods on his way back to Stonehurst Park late that afternoon.

If his neighbours had been surprised to receive a visit from the Duke of Rotherham then they had quickly masked the emotion, their manner effusive as they'd offered him tea and fancies.

Even when Felicity had been alive Griffin had always hated, had actively avoided, such visits.

The fact that he was now a widower, and an eligible duke at that, obviously had not escaped the notice of his neighbours. The Turners and the Howards had taken advantage of the opportunity to introduce him to any and all of their daughters who were of a marriageable age, the MacCawleys to a niece who was residing with them for the summer.

Only the Lathams had no daughter or niece

to thrust at him, and unfortunately they were away from home at present. The butler had informed him that Sir Walter, an avid member of the hunt, was currently in the next county looking to buy a promising grey, and his wife was away until the end of the week visiting friends.

Not that the latter was any great loss to Griffin; several inches taller than her rotund and jovial husband, Lady Francesca Latham was exactly the type of woman Griffin least admired. A blond-haired beauty, admittedly, but Lady Francesca also had a cold and sarcastic sense of humour, and spoke with a directness that Griffin found disconcerting, to say the least.

All of those visits had been a waste of his time and energy anyway, as he had not managed to ascertain any information from his conversations in regard to Bella, or Jacob Harker.

So the slowness of Griffin's pace on his journey back to Stonehurst Park was not due to any lingering enjoyment of his afternoon, but more out of a reluctance to see and be with Bella again.

He no longer trusted himself to be alone in her company.

The way he had responded to her earlier was unprecedented. He'd experienced a depth of arousal that had resulted in his continued discomfort for more than an hour after the two of them had parted. He had breathed a sigh of relief when she had asked to have her luncheon on a tray in her bedchamber, leaving him to dine alone in the small family dining room.

But Griffin knew he could not continue to avoid her. They would have to put those kisses behind them, by ignoring the incident, if by no other means. Although Griffin doubted he would be able to forget his response.

'Oh, thank goodness you are returned, Your Grace!'

A harried-looking Pelham came hurrying down the front steps of the house as Griffin dismounted and handed his reins to the waiting groom.

'There's been such a to-do! I did not know what to do for the best.'

'What is it, Pelham?' Griffin frowned his concern; Pelham had been butler here at

Stonehurst Park since Griffin was a boy, and as far as he was aware this was the first time he had seen the elderly man in the least discomposed.

'It is Miss Bella.'

'Bella?' Griffin quickly looked up towards the house. 'Has she fallen? Been injured in some way? Did someone come here while I was out?' he demanded belatedly. He knew someone would almost certainly be looking for Bella, following her escape, but Griffin had not thought they would dare to come here, to Stonehurst Park. 'Out with it, man!' he barked his impatience at his butler.

Pelham obviously did his best to calm himself, although there was still a light of panic in his eyes. 'We were just finished afternoon tea in the servants' dining room when we heard such a screaming and carry on.'

'Bella?' Griffin knew he was the one who was now less than composed. 'Did someone attack her? If someone has dared to harm her—'

'No, no, it is nothing like that, Your Grace. It seems that she must have fallen asleep some time after lunch, and had a nightmare. Mrs

Harcourt is up in her bedchamber with her now, but Miss Bella is inconsolable, and we did not know what to do for the best.'

Griffin was no longer there for the older man to explain the situation to; he was already ascending the front steps two at a time in his rush to get to Bella's side, throwing his hat aside as he hurried across the hallway to ascend the wide staircase just as hurriedly, all the time berating himself for having left Bella.

He should not have left her alone after all that she had so obviously suffered.

Nor should he have parted from her so angrily earlier, when *he* was the one who had been at fault for kissing her.

He was an unfeeling brute, who did not deserve—

'Griffin!'

He had barely stepped inside the bedchamber, his heart having contracted the moment he took in the sight of Bella's tear-stained face, when she jumped up suddenly from the bed to rush across the room and launch herself into his arms.

His own arms closed tightly about her as he

held her slenderness securely against him, feeling as he did the terrible trembling of her body.

'I am here now, Bella. I am here,' he assured her softly as she continued to sob and cling to him.

Her face was buried against his chest. 'It was…I was… It was so dark I could not see, only hear, and—'

'You may leave us now, Mrs Harcourt.' Griffin curtly dismissed the housekeeper; there was no need to add to the mystery of Bella's presence at Stonehurst Park. 'Perhaps you might have Pelham bring us up some tea in half an hour or so?' he added, to take the sting out of his dismissal as he saw the housekeeper's crestfallen expression.

'Yes, Your Grace.' She bobbed a curtsy before hurrying from the room, obviously as discomfited as Pelham by this upset.

'You are safe now, Bella,' Griffin assured her as he bent to swing her up in his arms and carry her across the bedchamber, where he sank down into the armchair, settling Bella on his knees as her body still shook uncontrollably.

She buried her face against the side of his throat. 'That is not my name.'

Griffin stroked a soothing hand down the length of her spine even as he lightly brushed the tangle of dark hair from her face. 'We have agreed it shall be for now.'

'No,' she sobbed emotionally. 'I meant that it really is not my name.' She raised her head and looked at him, eyes red, lashes damp, her cheeks flushed. 'I believe my—my real name is—I heard someone in my dream call me Beatrix.'

She had spent a miserable morning in her bedchamber, pacing up and down as she'd tried to decide what she should do for the best. What was best for Griffin, not herself.

He was so obviously a man who preferred his own company.

A singular gentleman, who did not care to involve himself in the lives of others.

A wealthy and eligible duke, who had not remarried after his duchess died six years ago.

And *she* was responsible for disturbing the constancy of his life.

What Bella *should* do now was leave here.

Remove herself from his home. Before news of a woman's presence at Stonehurst Park became known, as it surely would be if she remained here for any length of time. The last thing she wanted was to blacken Griffin's name.

Except she still had nowhere else to go, nor the means to get anywhere.

The tears of frustration she had cried had not helped to lessen the helplessness of Bella's situation in the slightest.

Any more than her best efforts to try not to think of the way Griffin had kissed her earlier. Or that he had called her a witch for having tempted him.

It had been in that state of despair and emotional turmoil that Bella had finally fallen into an exhausted asleep.

The dreams had seemed harmless at first. Just images, really. Of a smiling, laughing young lady, with fashionably styled dark hair, dressed in a beautiful gown of gold silk as she'd twirled about the room with another lady, older, but so like the first that they had to be mother and daughter. A seated gentleman had looked on and smiled at the two of them indulgently.

Then had come the overwhelming sadness as that image had faded and she'd seen the young lady again, dressed in black this time, her face ravaged by grief.

And she'd known, without a doubt, that the young woman in the dream was herself, and that she stood at the graveside of the same man and woman who had looked so happy in the previous image. She'd known instinctively that the man and woman were her father and her mother.

That image had faded to be replaced by hands reaching for her in the darkness. A hand placed over her mouth. The warning not to scream, before something, a cloth of some kind, had been placed over her mouth and her eyes, and she'd been dragged kicking from her bed before something had hit her on the side of the head and she'd known no more.

She had tried then to wake herself from the terror she'd felt, but she had not succeeded, that terror only increasing as instead the next image had been of waking to the painful jolting of a travelling carriage as she'd lain huddled and bound on the hard floor, unable to see, speak or move.

Even so, she'd known she was not alone in the carriage, had been able to smell an unwashed body and hear another person breathing, sometimes snoring, as they'd slept, but never speaking, except when the carriage had stopped and she had been dragged outside and told to relieve herself. She had refused at first, having had no idea where she was or who was watching her, but had roughly been warned she would be left in her own mess if she did not do as she was told.

The dream gave her no idea of time, of how long she had been in the carriage when it had finally stopped and she'd been dragged outside. There had been the sound of a door opening and closing, a degree of warmth, before she had been pushed to the floor and she'd felt ropes being twined about her wrists and ankles as she had been secured in place. The cloth about her mouth had been ripped away and she'd gagged as some stale bread had been pushed between her cracked and dry lips, followed by blessedly cool water.

She'd had images then of being forced to eat more stale bread, followed by that delicious cold water.

Even the smell of unwashed bodies had become normal as the time had passed and she'd known herself to be a part of that smell. As all she'd known had been that fear and hunger and cold. Until her jailer had been joined by another. And that was when the pain had begun.

The man's rough voice would ask her questions, and another person, someone who remained absolutely silent, had administered the kicks and slaps when she'd failed to give them the answers they'd seemed to want from her.

All that had existed for Bella was sitting alone in the darkness, being forced to eat the stale bread and water, followed by those questions being repeated over and over again. Followed by the painful kicks and slaps. The abuse had been accompanied by the harsh warnings of the first jailer when Bella had cried out that she did not understand the questions let alone have the answers they wanted.

Her nightmare, if it was a nightmare, and

not actually a memory, had seemed to go on endlessly. Pain, cold and hunger.

Until Bella had finally awoken to the sound of her own screams as she'd sat up in the bed. Those feelings still with her even though she was now fully awake; the shaking of her body beyond her control.

Pelham had burst through the bedchamber door first, quickly followed by the housekeeper, the two of them doing all that they could to soothe and calm her.

Except Bella could not be calmed or soothed. Not once she'd accepted that she had not been dreaming. That they were memories that had returned to her.

Along with the knowledge that her beloved parents were both dead.

So what did her captors want?

What did she overhear?

Who had she told?

Tell me, tell me, tell me!

She sat up suddenly, eyes wide as she turned to look at a grim-faced Griffin. 'Jacob,' she breathed harshly. 'The man who held me prisoner was called Jacob!'

Chapter Five

❦

Bella's, or rather Beatrix's, gasped statement was not what Griffin had been expecting to hear.

She had been so caught up in her nightmares still, so lost in those awful memories, that Griffin was sure she did not realise she had been talking out loud the whole time as she'd recounted the details of the visions that had caused her to wake screaming.

And as she'd remembered Griffin had felt himself becoming angrier and angrier at all she had suffered. It was a cold and vengeful anger, which he knew would only be assuaged when he found, and punished, the two people responsible for having treated Beatrix so cruelly.

Yet hadn't he also been guilty of mistreating her? By refusing to trust her and treating her with suspicion?

Admittedly, his many years as an agent for the Crown had created a deep cynicism and distrust within him. To the point where he was now wary of anyone who was not family or a close friend. This left him with a very small circle of people: his grandmother, the Dangerous Dukes and their wives, and Aubrey Maystone. And recent events had only added to his distrust and wariness.

However, was it possible that she was innocently involved in his own reason for being in Lancashire? 'Jacob?' he repeated softly. 'Could this man you refer to possibly be called Jacob Harker?'

She gave a pained frown. 'I never heard his last name, only his first, and I believe even that was by accident.'

'Can you describe him?' Griffin prompted gently. 'Did he have any distinguishing marks? A scar, perhaps? Or a mole?' Recalling that Harker had a mole on the left side of his neck.

She shuddered. 'I never saw him.'

Griffin frowned his puzzlement. 'I do not understand.'

'Usually there was a blindfold secured back and over my ears. On the day I heard his name they had been questioning me again, and had not covered my ears sufficiently, so that I could hear a muffled conversation, more like an argument, between the two of them outside of where I was kept prisoner.' She swallowed. 'The second jailer was angry, and remonstrating with the first, I think because they had once again failed to get the answers from me they wanted. One shouted that I would be dead before they had their answers. That is when I overheard one of them refer to the other as Jacob.'

Complete deprivation of sight, sound and touch, along with a minimum of food and water, with the added threat of dying a painful death; it was a standard method of torture.

That those things had been done to this helpless young woman made Griffin feel positively murderous.

If her parents were both dead, then where was her guardian, her closest male relative?

Someone, somewhere had surely been entrusted with the care of her after her parents' deaths? Whoever they were they deserved to be shot for their negligence.

Of course young ladies did sometimes run away in the middle of the night during or after the London season, but usually they returned several days or weeks later, either in disgrace or with a husband!

There was always the possibility that her guardians believed she had eloped.

'Bella—Beatrix?' Griffin hesitated over the name.

'Bea,' she corrected flatly. 'I believe my parents referred to me as Bea.'

Griffin did not miss the past tense in that statement, or the look of pained bewilderment in Bea's eyes. A pained bewilderment that he perfectly understood if, in fact, her parents were both dead, as she had dreamt they were. 'Do you remember them?'

'Only in the dream,' she answered dully. 'And only that one instance, when I was dancing giddily with my mother.'

That was, Griffin now strongly suspected,

because shock and fear were responsible for causing her amnesia. The memories were obviously returning to her, even if only subconsciously, but her imprisonment, the harshness of her treatment, meant it would probably take time for all of her memories from before her abduction to return to her completely.

He might have wished she could forget her imprisonment and torture too!

Griffin's attempts today, to see if Bea belonged to a family in the area, had come to naught.

On his way out this afternoon he had instructed Reynolds, his estate manager, to check on any of the empty cottages and woodcutters' sheds within the estate, in the hopes that he might find some sign of where Bea might have been held prisoner. Her flight through the woods the previous night surely meant that Bea could not have run far dressed as she was and without footwear.

Bea.

How strange that he had chosen a name for her not so far from her own.

Tears dampened her lashes as she pulled

abruptly out of his arms before standing up. 'I do not know how or when my parents died, but it must have been recently I think, because in my dream I attended their funeral, and I did not look so different then, except for the bruises, from how I am now.' The tears fell unchecked down the pallor of her hollowed cheeks.

'I am sorry for that, Bea,' Griffin consoled as he stood up to go to her, taking a light grasp of her arms as he looked down at her. 'I am so very sorry for your loss.'

'I do not remember them.' She shook her head sadly as she drew her bottom lip between her teeth in an effort to stop any more tears from falling. 'I only know of them at all because I saw myself standing at their gravesides, and knew that I loved and grieved for them both.'

How Bea had survived, even as well as she had, after all that had recently been done to her, Griffin could not even begin to comprehend.

She might have survived physically, he corrected himself grimly, but emotionally it was a different matter. It appeared now that Bea's mind had simply shut itself down and refused to remember.

Except in her dreams.

But the things that Bea had now recalled about herself in those dreams were something Griffin might use in order to further try and identify who she was. She was obviously well spoken and educated, which indicated that in all likelihood her parents had been also. A further adage to that was they had, in all probability, been members of society; there could not be too many couples in society who had both died at the same time, and recently, and with a daughter named Beatrix.

Being so far away from London himself, Griffin now knew he had no choice but to write to Aubrey Maystone and ask him to look into the matter for him.

'Bea, I hate having to ask you to dwell on this any further just now, but...'

'If I have the answer I will gladly give it,' Bea assured him sadly, the grief, the dark oppression of her dreams, obviously still weighing her down.

He nodded. 'The questions the man Jacob asked. What were they?'

'They were the same two questions, over and over again. How much did I overhear? Who had I told?' She frowned as she gave a shake of her head. 'I did not know the answers then, and I do not know them now.'

Griffin realised that someone obviously *believed* that she knew something they would rather she did not.

And it was in all possibility something to do with the reason why Jacob Harker had left Northamptonshire so suddenly several weeks ago, and travelled up to Lancashire.

Something of relevance to the foiled assassination plot of the Prince Regent just weeks ago?

Harker's possible involvement in Bea's abduction would seem to imply that was in all probability the case.

Griffin filed the information away in his head. 'How did you finally manage to escape?'

She frowned. 'The man, Jacob, had taken to unfastening my hands and feet when I was allowed to use—' She gave a shake of her head, her cheeks becoming flushed. 'I believe I struck him on the side of the head with the bucket before ripping off my blindfold and simply running and running. Does this man, Jacob, mean something to you?' She looked up at him sharply.

Griffin frowned grimly. 'It is not important.'

'It is important to *me*!' Some of her earlier fire returned as her eyes flashed darkly.

Griffin gentled his voice. 'I believe the best thing for now would be for you to rest.'

'No!' Bea pulled out of the Duke's grasp before stepping back. 'I cannot. I do not wish to rest.' Even the thought of going to sleep again, of having more nightmares, was enough to fill her with panic. 'I should like to know what relevance this man Jacob Harker has to you. Why, upon hearing the name Jacob, did you immediately assume he might be this Harker you speak of?'

'He is a known troublemaker in the area, that is all,' Griffin soothed.

Bea was not fooled for a moment by that explanation. 'That still does not explain why—'

'Bell—Bea,' he corrected apologetically. 'It

is not the best time for us to talk about him, when you are already so upset.' He looked grim. 'I am more interested in the questions that were asked of you, and what significance they— Damn it!' he muttered in frustration as there was a brief knock on the bedchamber door. 'We will talk of this again once we are alone again.'

'I really do not think I can discuss my actual imprisonment any more just now, Griffin.' Her voice broke emotionally. 'It is too—distressing.' She was slightly ashamed of this show of weakness on her part, but was unable, for the moment, to think any more of her imprisonment and what her dreams had already revealed.

Her worst fear now—a fear she dared not talk of out loud—was that she might also have been violated.

She did not remember it, did not feel in the least sore between her legs. But perhaps she would not have noticed that soreness amongst the other bruises, cuts and abrasions on her body?

Just the thought of that smelly and disgusting man laying so much as a finger on her—

The dreams, revelations, that she had already had, about her most recent life, before Griffin had found her in the woods last night, along with the things she had not yet remembered, made Bea's position here now seem even more precarious than it had been previously.

If that were possible.

She was an orphan. And one whom no one seemed to have claimed or loved, for if they had then surely her sudden disappearance would have caused a hue and cry, and in all likelihood Griffin would now know exactly who she was.

Instead of which he was obviously as much in the dark as to her identity as she was.

Although the name Jacob had certainly meant something to him. Something he did not wish to discuss with her.

'Come in, Pelham,' the Duke now instructed impatiently as a second knock sounded on the door. The door opened and the butler entered with the tray of tea things, quickly followed by the housekeeper carrying a large box.

'Some of Miss Bella's gowns, Your Grace,' she explained hastily as the Duke scowled at her presence.

'My goddaughter would prefer that we call her Bea in future,' Griffin announced haughtily.

Earlier today Bea had been almost excited at the prospect of new gowns, ones that actually fitted her. But the events since had reduced their arrival to mediocrity.

And Griffin's claim now, that she was his goddaughter, further robbed her of speech.

Although she appreciated that their present situation must be as awkward for him as it was for her. If not more so.

He was a duke, and a widower, and this was his primary ducal estate, and Bea's dreams now indicated they would not discover who she was, or to what family she belonged, as quickly as he might have hoped. Bea could hardly continue to stay here without some further offer of explanation being made to his household staff as to the reason for her sudden presence in their employer's home.

But surely her late arrival last night with

the Duke, wearing only her soiled nightgown, gave instant lie to the claim she was his god-daughter?

If Pelham or Mrs Harcourt found his choice of explanation in the least surprising, then they gave no indication of it. The butler placed the tray of tea things on the table in front of the window, and the housekeeper placed the box containing Bea's new gowns on the bed, both acknowledging their employer respectfully before departing the bedchamber.

'I am sorry I could not pre-warn you of my announcement, Bea.' He grimaced ruefully once they were alone together. 'As I am sure you can appreciate, following this afternoon's upset, some further explanation for your presence here now has to be given.'

As Bea also knew, without his having to say it, that Griffin was a man who disliked intensely having to explain himself to anyone.

As the powerful and wealthy Duke of Rotherham he no doubt rarely felt the need to do so!

Except Bea needed some further explanations herself.

Since waking she had several times thought of her dishevelled state when Griffin had found her the previous night. 'Who undressed and bathed me last night, and then dressed me in a clean nightgown?' she prompted slowly; she had certainly not been wearing the soiled or bloodstained garment from her dreams when she woke this morning.

'I did,' he dismissed briskly. 'I thought it best that none of my household staff be made privy to your bruises or abrasions,' he added abruptly as Bea's eyes widened.

Instead this breathtakingly handsome man had undressed her before bathing her completely naked body.

That he had seen her in that dirty and disgusting state was humiliating enough. To think of him stripping her, washing her, and then dressing her in a clean nightgown was far too intimate to contemplate.

'And my old nightgown?'

'I gave it to Pelham and instructed him to burn it this morning,' Griffin said coolly. 'Do not look so aghast, Bea; Pelham has been at Stonehurst Park for most of my life. He is and always has been the height of discretion, and you may rest assured he will not discuss the matter with anyone else.'

Bea was far more concerned with Griffin having seen her total humiliation, her unwashed and bruised body, than she was with the kindly butler's sensibilities.

She kept her eyes downcast as she turned away to look at the laden tea tray, noting the two cups and saucers. 'Will you be joining me for tea?'

'I think not, thank you,' Griffin refused stiffly, accepting that Bea was unwilling to discuss this any further just now, and knowing it was past time he removed himself from her bedchamber.

Despite her earlier upset, and his claim now of being her godfather, it was still not acceptable that he spend so much time alone with her in her bedchamber.

Even if a part of him wished to do so.

Being reminded of the intimacy of bathing her the night before, of kissing her, and holding her in his arms, listening as she talked of the nightmares, Griffin felt the tenuous strands of an emotional bond being forged between the two of them.

And it would not do.

He was not truly Bea's godfather, but a healthy and virile man of two and thirty who was totally unrelated to her, and who had several times responded to her in a physical way that was definitely not in the least godfatherly!

They did not as yet know Bea's true circumstances or age, but Griffin now felt sure she came from a good family, and that he was at the very least ten years her senior.

He had suffered through an unhappy marriage, and his experiences with women these past six years had not lessened that disillusionment in the slightest. He was distrustful of them at best, cynical at worst.

He had once believed that Felicity felt an affection for him, and that the two of them would be together for the rest of their lives. He had been fond of Felicity, if not deeply in love with her, and totally faithful and loyal to their marriage. Both had been thrown back in his face when Felicity had chosen another man's affections and body over his own.

He would have to marry again one day, of course, if only to provide his heir, but Griffin was determined his second wife would be a woman for whom he held only respect, as the future mother of his children. Nor would he expect his duchess to feel any unwanted affection for him.

He had not been in the past, and he was not now, nor could he ever be, any young woman's romantic image of a knight in shining armour.

Still, at the moment he was sure Bea must feel a certain gratitude towards him, an emotion based solely on his having rescued her the previous evening.

As such, his own physical response to her, as well as his growing feelings for her, were both totally inappropriate.

'We will meet again at dinner, if you feel up to joining me downstairs?' he asked coolly.

Did Bea feel up to bathing and dressing in one of her new gowns before joining him for dinner?

It would certainly be a *normal* activity, in a world that now seemed even more alien to her than it had before. Besides which, her afternoon spent alone had resulted in those mind-numbing nightmares, and she wished to avoid the possibility of experiencing any more of those for as long as was possible.

'Dinner downstairs would be lovely, thank you,' she accepted equally coolly, fully intending to ask Pelham if she might have a bath before then. She felt unclean after the vividness of her dreams, as if some of that filth and squalor in which she had been kept prisoner still clung to her.

Griffin gave her a formal bow. 'Until eight o'clock, then.'

Bea kept her lashes lowered demurely as she gave a curtsy, and remained so until she heard the door quietly closing as Griffin left her bedchamber.

At which time she released a heavily sighing breath.

Her dreams had truly been nightmares.

Her fragmented memories, of her parents, her abduction and imprisonment, the frantic madness of her flight from her jailer, were even more so.

And there was still that lingering doubt that

she might have been physically violated by her captors.

If so, was it possible she might have buried that particular horrific memory so deep inside her it might never show itself again?

Until such time as she married and her husband discovered she was not a virgin bride.

If she ever married.

And if she ever remembered who she truly was.

'You are looking very lovely this evening, Bea,' Griffin complimented politely once the two of them were seated opposite each other at the small round table in the family dining room.

Bea did indeed look very beautiful; the housekeeper had managed to find a gown the colour almost the same deep blue as her eyes. Her hair was fashionably styled upon her crown, with several enticing curls at her temples and nape. She was a little pale still, but that only added to her delicacy of appearance, which bordered on ethereal.

Griffin felt heartily relieved that it was not

yet dark enough for Pelham to light the candles in the centre of the table; a romantic candlelit dinner for two would be the height of folly in the circumstances.

'Thank you,' she accepted lightly. 'You are looking very handsome this evening too.'

They sounded like polite acquaintances passing the time as their dinner was served, when in reality they were far from that. After leaving Bea earlier he had gone immediately to the library to send an urgent letter to Maystone, prompting the other man to use his considerable influence and acquaintances to ascertain any and all information he could about a missing young lady named Beatrix.

It would take several days but Griffin had felt better in the knowledge he had at least done something positive in that regard.

His estate manager had also asked to see him earlier, as he believed one of the disused woodcutters' sheds in Shrawley Woods might have recently been inhabited. Griffin had immediately ridden out to look for himself.

It was situated about a mile from where Griffin had found Bea, and whoever had stayed in the barely furnished shed had attempted to cover their tracks. But it was impossible to hide the stench of unwashed bodies, or the presence of a bloodstained bucket in the corner of one of the downstairs rooms—the same bucket Bea had struck Jacob Harker about the head with?

Griffin believed it was and his rage had grown tenfold as he'd stood and looked about him. The shed consisted of just two rooms, the floors were of dirt, just a single broken chair and table in one of the rooms, and no other furniture. The roof overhead sagged, and no doubt leaked in several places too. Several dark rags had been draped over the single square cut out of one of the wooden walls. No doubt to prevent anyone from looking in. Or out.

There was nothing else there to show recent habitation, no ragged blankets, fresh food or water, but it was impossible to miss the recent odour of unwashed bodies, or the stench of rotting food.

And the distinctive smell of fear.

Bea's fear...

Griffin had given Reynolds a grim-faced nod before leaving the shed to ride back alone to Stonehurst Park, an impotent rage burning deep within him. And as he'd ridden the heavens had opened up, as if the angels themselves cried for all that Bea had suffered.

He had not told her as yet that he believed he had discovered the place of her imprisonment, and he was not sure that he intended to. She appeared so composed this evening, and was so elegantly attired, and Griffin had no wish to disturb that composure by once again taking her thoughts back to her imprisonment.

It was impossible to deny it had happened, of course; Griffin could still see some of the bruises on her shoulders and arms, although she had attempted to fasten a cream lace shawl over them in an effort to hide the worst of the abuse she had suffered. Matching lace gloves covered her bandaged wrists, and the length of her gown covered her bandaged ankles.

Covering signs of her abuse that once again incited Griffin's displeasure.

'I will ring for you when we have finished eating our soup,' he tersely dismissed Pelham, finding even the butler's quiet presence in the room to be an intrusion.

Griffin realised his mistake as soon as the older man left the room as the intimacy of earlier suddenly fell over the two of them like a cloak.

Bea knew a sudden discomfort at being alone with her dashing Duke. Well, he was not *her* Duke. Griffin was most certainly his own man. Self-contained, aloof, and demanding of respect. But he *was* her very handsome rescuer, and several times Bea had sensed an awareness between the two of them that was not avuncular. And earlier today he had kissed her.

'The soup is delicious,' she remarked to fill the sudden silence.

'My cook here is very good.' He smiled slightly, as if aware of her discomfort.

Because he felt it also? Bea would be very surprised if too much discomforted this confident gentleman.

'Thank you for my new gowns.' There had been three gowns in the box Mrs Harcourt had brought to her bedchamber earlier, two day dresses and one for the evening, the blue gown Bea was now wearing, along with undergarments, a shawl and slippers. 'I hope—I hope that once I am restored to—to being myself again, that I shall be in a position to repay you.'

'A few second-hand gowns altered by the local seamstress will not bankrupt my estate, Bea!' the Duke rasped impatiently.

'Nevertheless.' Bea was not to be gainsaid on the subject; she had taken enough from this gentleman already, in the form of his kindness and hospitality, and she did not intend to be indefinitely in his debt financially too.

Griffin frowned his irritation with this conversation. 'You must concentrate your energies on becoming completely well again, and not worry yourself over such trivialities.'

Her chin rose. 'I assure you, they are not trivial to me.'

Griffin eyed her curiously. 'I have a feeling that, whatever your true identity might be, you are an independent and determined young lady!'

The fullness of her lips curved into a rueful smile. 'I would hope so.'

Griffin was sure that she was. He believed that many young women who had been as ill treated as Bea had would now be prostrate with the vapours. And possibly remain so for many days. Bea might feel that way inside, but outwardly she was calm and collected.

'You have the courage and fortitude of a queen,' he complimented huskily as he all too easily pictured the hovel in which she had been kept prisoner.

A blush slowly warmed her cheeks, lashes lowered over her eyes. 'I do not feel like a queen.'

Griffin looked at her searchingly. 'Something else is troubling you.' It was a statement, not a question. 'What is it, Bea?' he asked sharply. 'Have you remembered something else?'

Tears glistened in her eyes as she looked at him. 'It is what I do not remember that now troubles me.'

'Such as?'

She gave an abrupt shake of her head, no longer meeting his gaze.

'I would rather not put it into words.'

Griffin frowned darkly. Bea had been physically beaten, emotionally tortured, what else could there possibly be to—? 'No, Bea!' he gasped harshly. 'Surely you do not think—? Do not believe—?'

'Why should I not think that?' Bea dropped her spoon noisily into her bowl as she gave up all pretence of eating. 'I was alone with these men, and at their complete mercy for goodness knows how long. Surely in those circumstances it would be foolhardy to assume that—that one did not—' She could not finish the sentence, could not put into words this last possible horror of her captivity.

Once it had been thought of, Bea had been unable to put the possibility of physical violation from her mind. She had tried to appear calm as she'd joined Griffin in the dining room. Had been determined not to speak of her worries with him.

But the what-ifs had continued to haunt her. To plague her.

Until it seemed it was all she could think of.

Griffin also looked suitably horrified at the possibility of violation as he now placed one of his hands firmly over both of her trembling ones clasped tightly together on her thighs. 'Bea, I am sure that did not happen.'

'You are no surer than I am!' she instantly rebutted, eyes glittering. 'I want these men found, Griffin. I want Jacob found and the truth beaten from him if he will not give it any other way!' Two bright spots of fevered colour heated her cheeks.

'Bea!'

'If you will excuse me, Griffin?' She pulled her hands away from his and threw her napkin on the tabletop before standing up noisily from the table. 'I do not believe I am hungry, after all.' She turned on her heel and almost ran from the room.

Griffin sat alone at the dining table, once again at a loss to know what to do where Bea was concerned.

Should he go after her and offer her more words of comfort?

Or should he leave her alone and allow her time to come to terms with her thoughts?

Was Griffin himself not in need of several minutes in which to fully take in the shocking implication of Bea's suspicion regarding her treatment at the hands of the man called Jacob?

Chapter Six

Bea found it impossible to fall sleep. She was *afraid* to fall asleep. For fear that more of those dreams might come back to haunt her. For fear that she might learn more from those dreams than she was comfortable knowing...

So instead of sleeping, she threw back the dishevelled bedclothes and paced her bedchamber long after she had heard Griffin pass her door, no doubt on the way to his own bedchamber further down the hallway.

What must he now think of her?

Nothing she did not think of herself, Bea felt sure!

Of course, she was not to blame if she had been violated, but that would not make it any less true. Any less of a disgrace. Whether she had been forced or otherwise, it would not change the fact that Bea was no longer—

Bea raised her hands and pressed her palms tightly against each of her temples, sure she would go mad if she did not stop this circle of thought from going constantly round and round inside her head.

It felt as if there were no longer any air in her bedchamber for her to breathe!

Not enough room in here for her.

She needed to flee.

To escape!

'I believe you are safer, here with me, than you would be anywhere else, Bea.'

She had no sooner thrown open her bed-chamber door and stepped out into the hallway, her nightgown billowing about her bare legs, her hair loose about her shoulders and down her back, when she came to a halt at the sound of Griffin's calm and reasoning voice.

Her eyes widened as she turned and saw him leaning casually back against the pale pink silk-covered wall just a short distance down the hallway.

He had removed his jacket, but still wore the

rest of his evening clothes. He somehow looked younger now that he was less formally clothed, and with the darkness of his hair tousled on his brow, his grey eyes heavy with exhaustion.

Bea eyed him uncertainly. 'I thought you had gone to your bedchamber some time ago.'

'I did.' Griffin straightened away from the wall to walk down the hallway towards her, his movements as silent and graceful as a large cat's. 'But I heard you pacing and muttering to yourself as I walked past your bedchamber, and guessed that you would find it difficult to sleep tonight. That you would perhaps have thoughts of running away?' He came to a halt just inches in front of her, hooded lids preventing Bea from seeing the expression. 'The things you remember suffering are bad enough on their own, Bea. Do not torture yourself further with thoughts of something that might not have happened.'

Tears stung her eyes as she gave a shake of her head. 'That is all well and good for you to say, Griffin, but you cannot possibly understand.'

'Bea, I was once held prisoner myself.'

'You were?' She blinked up at him uncertainly as he spoke quietly.

'I was captured by the French after the battle of Talavera,' he admitted grimly; it was not a time he normally chose to talk about. To anyone. And yet he knew that he had to. That it was his only way of assuring Bea that he knew a little of how she was feeling tonight. 'I do not pretend to understand the devils tormenting you, but I know what it is like to lose your freedom, to have suffered physical torture. To know of the scars it leaves on the soul.'

'How long were you held prisoner?'

He shrugged. 'A week or so, until I too escaped. What I am really saying, Bea, is that we all carry scars about with us we have acquired from life, whether they be physical or emotional.'

Bea felt shame wash over her at learning Griffin had been held a prisoner of the French in the war against Napoleon. She had also forgotten, caught up in her own self-pity as she had been, that Griffin must grieve still for his dead wife, making her doubly ashamed at her own self-indulgence.

'Life can be so cruel!' She rested her forehead against Griffin's wide and muscled chest, at once able to feel his reassuring warmth through the material of his waistcoat and shirt, and the steady, comforting beat of his heart. 'Truth be told, I am afraid to fall asleep,' she admitted huskily.

'Understandably.' Griffin's arms moved about her as he held her close against him.

She could not seem to stop the trembling. 'I— Would you—? Could you possibly sit with me for a while? Knowing you are there, and that I am safe, perhaps I will sleep and not dream?'

Griffin tensed at the request, knowing that his self-control was not at a premium where Bea was concerned. Just holding her in his arms like this, being completely aware of her nakedness beneath her nightgown, of her beautiful silky dark hair flowing loose down the length of her spine, was sorely testing that control.

At the same time he knew that it would be cruel of him to deny Bea this small comfort. He had already borne witness to her distress this afternoon, following her nightmares. The concern she had voiced earlier, about what else might have happened to her, disturbed him almost as much as it did her.

The thought of any man—*any man*—laying hands on Bea, let alone the animals who had kept her a prisoner in such filthy conditions, who had abused her both emotionally and physically, was enough to fill Griffin with a murderous rage.

His hands now closed into fists as he fought against that anger, knowing that it served no purpose right now; Bea needed his reassurance, not his rage.

The time for Griffin to let loose the full extent of his fury would come if—*when*—he caught up with Jacob Harker.

Because he would find him. And when he did the other man would suffer as he had made Bea suffer.

'Of course,' he now agreed briskly. 'What else are godfathers for?' he added lightly, and knowing he was deliberately using that tenuous claim in the hopes of amusing her, but also as a means of attempting to place their relationship on a platonic footing.

As a means of convincing himself that his feelings towards Bea were indeed platonic.

A husky laugh caught in Bea's throat as she straightened. 'I believe I shall like having you for my godfather.'

Griffin had never felt less like someone's godfather—Bea's godfather, in particular— than he did as he followed her inside her bedchamber and closed the door behind them.

A single candle burned on the bedside table to alleviate the darkness of the room, the bedclothes badly rumpled from where Bea had obviously gone to bed earlier, but had only tossed and turned, before rising again when she had been unable to sleep. When she had been too afraid to sleep, Griffin corrected himself grimly.

He moved to briskly straighten the bedclothes before turning them back invitingly. 'Ready?'

Bea felt more than a little self-conscious now that they were alone together in the silent intimacy of her bedchamber, the very air about them seeming to have stilled.

Almost with expectation?

She kept her gaze averted as she climbed back into bed, laying her head back on the pillows as Griffin rearranged the covers over her and tucked them beneath her chin. Bea almost expected him to place a fatherly kiss upon her brow!

When her own feelings towards him were far from paternal.

Griffin, instead of kissing her brow, now moved to carry the chair over from the window and place it beside the bed, before folding his long length down into it as he sat down beside her.

What would they have thought of each other if they had met under normal circumstances, at a society ball, or perhaps a musical soirée?

Bea almost laughed as she asked herself that question; even if Griffin were to ever attend such frivolities, which she seriously doubted, then she did not believe he would have noticed her existence.

Just as she had absolutely no doubt that she

most certainly *would* have noticed Griffin, whatever the circumstances of their meeting!

He had such presence, was so tall and handsome, it would be impossible for any woman not to notice, or to be attracted to the charismatic Duke of Rotherham.

And yet he had never remarried.

Because he had loved his wife so much the idea of marriage to another woman repulsed him?

That had to be the explanation, Bea accepted wistfully.

Oh, but it would have been so wonderful to meet Griffin under different circumstances. For him to have asked to dance with her at a ball. To have him accompany her into supper. To have him call or send flowers the following day.

Bea brought her thoughts up sharply as she realised that all of those things seemed perfectly natural to her. That perhaps they had happened in her previous life?

Oh, not with Griffin, more was the pity, but she was sure she had danced at balls, and been accompanied into suppers by handsome gentlemen, and that they had called or sent flowers the following day.

Slowly, too slowly for Bea's peace of mind, her memories seemed to be returning to her.

Griffin sat quiet and unmoving as he watched Bea slowly relax, her lids fluttering and then falling softly downwards, dark lashes caressing the paleness of her cheeks, her lips slightly parted, as she fell asleep.

He breathed out a soft and relieved sigh as he relaxed back into the same uncomfortable chair in which he had dozed fitfully the previous night. Sitting at Bea's bedside seemed to be becoming something of a habit! He continued to watch her for several minutes longer, before his own lack of sleep the night before finally caught up with him and he lay his head back against the chair and fell asleep himself.

Bea woke to the feel of the warmth of the sun caressing her cheeks, and a deeper warmth down the left side of her body, and with a not uncomfortable weight across her abdomen and her legs. Almost as if—

She quickly opened her eyes, slowly turning

her head to the left as she looked beside her, her breath catching in her throat as she saw that Griffin lay next to her, one of his arms curved about her waist, a leg thrown over the top of both of hers.

As if he were protecting her, even in his sleep.

He lay above the covers rather than under them, Bea discovered on closer inspection, the darkness of his hair more tousled than ever as his head lay on the pillows beside her own, his harshly chiselled features appearing much softer in sleep.

Bea's fingers itched to trace those finely arched brows. The sharply etched cheeks and the length of his aristocratic nose. As for those chiselled lips…

They looked so much softer when Griffin's mouth was not set in the habitually grim and determined shape it bore when he was awake. Lips so soft and inviting, in fact, that Bea's temptation to taste them became too much for her, her lids fluttering closed as she began to move her face closer towards his.

'What are you doing?'

Bea froze with her own lips just inches away from Griffin's, guilty colouring warming her cheeks as she looked up at him; she had been so intent on kissing the softness of his lips, she had failed to notice that Griffin had raised his own lids and was now looking at her with stormy grey eyes.

Angry eyes?

She moistened her own parted lips before answering him. 'I was…merely taken aback at finding you here in bed beside me.' She turned the explanation into a challenge, having no intention of owning up to the yearning she had known to kiss him, to taste the soft temptation of his lips.

Lips that were once again set in that grim, uncompromising line as he sat up in the bed before swinging his legs to the floor and standing up.

'I apologise,' he rasped gruffly as he looked down at her between narrowed lids, his back stiff and unyielding, shoulders tensed. He had removed his boots, and unbuttoned his waistcoat, but otherwise was still as fully dressed as he had been the night before. 'I meant only to hold you for several minutes after your upset, and that blasted chair is so uncomfortable.' He scowled at the offending piece of furniture. 'I must have drifted off to sleep myself once you were settled.'

Only one part of that explanation held any significance for Bea. 'After my upset?' Her face paled at the thought she might have had another nightmare. One that might possibly have revealed even more of the events of her captivity.

'You did not wake, just became restless and disturbed, and muttered a little in your sleep.' Griffin frowned as he recalled how he had been woken from his own fitful dozing in the chair in the early hours of the morning to see Bea thrashing restlessly in the bed, her words incomprehensible to him as she muttered and protested and cried out in her sleep.

Except for…

He looked down at her searchingly. 'Who is Michael?'

Bea returned his gaze blankly, her face unnaturally pale.

'Michael?' she repeated uncertainly.

'Michael,' Griffin confirmed abruptly. 'You called out for him in your sleep.'

'I did?' Her expression remained uncomprehending.

He nodded. 'You kept repeating his name, and then you said, "Michael must be so alone, so very alone!" and then you began to cry.'

Griffin could still remember the clenching of his gut as Bea had called out for the other man in her sleep, and how she had shed tears because she could not be with him.

He had no memory of having fallen asleep on the bed beside her after he had sought to comfort her, but he did recall the weight of her obvious love for the other man as weighing heavily on his chest.

Because he had enjoyed kissing her?

Because he wanted to kiss her again?

Because he was growing fond of Bea himself?

Griffin briskly dismissed such thoughts as nonsense. He merely felt responsible for Bea, and was concerned as to what had happened to her and why. Saddened for her, too, because she seemed to be so alone in the world.

Except she obviously was not as alone as he had thought she was. Because she was obviously concerned for—loved?—a man named Michael.

Did this Michael love her in return?

Of course he did; how could any man not fall in love with Bea if she chose to give her love to him?

Then where was this Michael now?

Why was he not the one here to comfort Bea when she was so lost and in pain? And why was he not ripping the country apart in his efforts to find her? To rescue her?

As Griffin was sure he would have done, in the same circumstances!

An obvious answer to those questions was that perhaps the other man was dead.

That the reason this Michael was not searching for Bea was because the people who had taken her might possibly have killed her lover during that abduction? It might even be that it was the shock of that death that was responsible for her amnesia, rather than the blow she had received to the head, or the horror of her abduction.

Bea gave a shake of her head, tears glistening in her eyes. 'I do not recall knowing anyone named Michael. Who could he be?' she added agitatedly.

'Please do not upset yourself, Bea.' Griffin heard the clock out in the hallway striking the hour of six. 'I believe I must now return to my own bedchamber.' He grimaced. 'The maid will arrive with my morning tea very shortly, and my valet not long after, to prepare my bath and lay out my clothes.'

'I— Of course.' Bea blinked. 'I have inconvenienced you far too much already, without the added scandal of your being found in my bedchamber at this hour, and in a state of undress.'

It would certainly be a first in this house for Griffin to be found in any lady's bedchamber in the morning, he acknowledged grimly. Even in the early days of their marriage Felicity had rarely allowed him entry to her bedchamber, and when she did she had always insisted that he leave again immediately after one of their less than satisfactory couplings, with the claim that she could not possibly fall asleep with his bulk in the bed beside her.

As Bea had done so easily and comfortably the night before.

And making comparisons of the way in which the two women regarded him was not only unproductive but also painful. It was like comparing night and day, rain or shine, when Bea was so obviously daylight and sunshine, after the dark and stormy years of being Felicity's barely tolerated husband.

His mouth tightened at those memories. 'I really do have to go now.' For the sake of his sanity, if nothing else! 'We will talk of this further over breakfast, if you wish.' He gave a terse bow before collecting up his boots and departing the room.

Bea was left momentarily stunned at the abruptness with which Griffin had left her. She felt guilty as she realised how her presence here was a constant inconvenience to him. Firstly, by his being forced into the position of becoming her saviour at all. And latterly, her presence here, an unaccompanied and young lady, surely bringing his reputation into question within his own household.

And who could this man Michael be? Someone she obviously felt an affection for, if she was calling out for him in her sleep. Perhaps he was a brother or other relative? Or a fiancé?

The thought of a fiancé caused Bea to go cold inside.

She had only known Griffin for a day, but it had been a significant and highly emotional time. And her attraction to him, her physical response to his having kissed her, her complete trust in him, could not be denied.

So perhaps her restlessness last night, her calling out for this man named Michael, had been because of a guilty conscience on her part, because she now found herself so inexplicably drawn to the man who had become her rescuer?

Whatever the reason, she resolved to be as little of a burden to Griffin as was possible in the coming days.

And nights.

* * *

'Sir Walter Latham has called to see you, Your Grace.'

Griffin looked up from the papers on his desk to first look at Pelham and then to glance frowningly across his study at Bea, as she sat curled up in a chair beside the fire reading a book. He noted pleasurably how the afternoon sun made her hair appear a particularly beautiful shade of blue-black against the pale lemon of her gown.

These past three days had been surprisingly companionable ones, with just the two of them sitting here together in the library during the day, he working on estate business, Bea quietly engrossed in her book, before they dined together in the evenings. Their conversations together had flowed surprisingly easily, Bea proving to be an intelligent woman, knowledgeable and able to discuss many subjects, despite her continued lack of memories of her own former life.

Much as Griffin had once imagined he would spend tranquil days and quiet evenings at home with his wife. Except Felicity had never wanted to sit companionably with him anywhere. In fact, towards the end of their marriage, it had become almost too much to expect her to even occupy the same house as him.

He frowned as he once again firmly put thoughts of Felicity from his mind to turn and look at his butler standing in the doorway. 'Show Sir Walter into the blue salon, if you please, Pelham,' he instructed impatiently.

'Very good, Your Grace.' The butler bowed out of the room, closing the door quietly behind him.

'Sir Walter Latham?' Bea repeated curiously as she closed her book.

'A neighbour who was away from home when I called upon him three days ago,' Griffin dismissed as he stood up from behind his desk to pull on his jacket. 'He is obviously home again now and simply returning my visit to him. I think it might be for the best if you were to remain here while I speak with him.'

'Of course.' Bea readily agreed to the suggestion; she had absolutely no interest in meeting any of Griffin's neighbours.

People who would no doubt be curious as to who she was, and what she was doing here.

People who might know Griffin well enough to know that he did not have a goddaughter named Beatrix.

Although she was a little disappointed at having their tranquillity interrupted. A surprising tranquillity, considering the unusual manner in which they had first met, and the uncertainty that still surrounded Bea's past.

Her bruises were rapidly fading, and she no longer wore the bandages on her wrists and ankles, but unfortunately her memory beyond her abduction and imprisonment continued to remain elusively out of her reach.

By tacit agreement it seemed, the two of them had not referred again to Bea's disturbed dreams of three nights ago, or of her having called out for another man. Bea felt distinctly uncomfortable at the thought she might have a fiancé pining away for her somewhere, and Griffin was no doubt respecting her own silence on the subject.

Consequently they had fallen into an easy routine during the past three days. Bea, in keeping with her decision not to be any more of a burden to Griffin than necessary, had chosen to suffer her sleepless nights in silence. Although she often fell asleep here in the library beside the fire during the daylight hours, reassured, no doubt, by Griffin's presence across the room.

'I am perfectly content to remain in here until after your visitor has gone,' she now assured him lightly.

'This should not take long.' He deftly straightened the cuffs of his white shirt beneath his jacket, looking every inch the Duke in his perfectly tailored dark grey superfine, black waistcoat, pale grey pantaloons and highly polished black Hessians. 'Amiable he might be, but one can only listen to so much of Sir Walter's conversation on the hunt and the magnificent horse flesh in his stable!' he added dryly.

Bea chuckled softly. 'He sounds a dear.'

Griffin considered the idea. 'He is most certainly one of the more congenial of my closest neighbours.'

'And is there also a Lady Latham?'

'She is something less than a dear,' Griffin

assured him with feeling, more than a little relieved that Lady Francesca appeared not to have returned as yet to accompany her husband on this visit to Stonehurst Park.

Why was it, he wondered, that amiable men such as Sir Walter more often than not burdened themselves with a controlling wife? An attraction of opposites, perhaps? Although Griffin could not claim to have ever seen much of that attraction in regard to Francesca Latham and Sir Walter!

'Would you like me to ask Pelham to bring you some tea in my absence?' he added briskly.

'That would be lovely, thank you.' Bea gave him a grateful smile.

Griffin drew in a deep breath as he felt himself bathed in the warm glow of that smile, before just as quickly giving himself an inner shake as he reminded himself that this current arrangement could only ever be a temporary one. That, in fact, he might not have the right to enjoy Bea's companionship at all, or to wallow in the warmth of her smiles.

That those things might all belong to a man called Michael.

Hopefully Aubrey Maystone would have received his letter by now, and might at this very moment be making the enquiries Griffin had requested, and thus soon putting an end to the mystery that was Bea.

Griffin's feelings on the subject had become mixed over these past three days. The longer Bea remained here at Stonehurst Park, the more he came to enjoy her company. At the same time it was foolish to do so, when at any moment her memories might come back to her, and she would then be returned to her former life, her time spent at Stonehurst Park, and with Griffin himself, both things she would rather put to the farthest reaches of her mind.

Griffin had ensured there had been no opportunity for a repeat of the kiss they had shared that first day, but that did not mean he did not feel desire every time he so much as looked at her.

A desire that Bea, so innocently trusting, obviously did not see or recognise.

Or return.

'I won't be long,' Griffin said harshly before turning sharply on his heel and leaving the room, instructing Pelham regarding Bea's tea, and striding determinedly into the blue salon to join Sir Walter.

At the same time as he determined he must put all thoughts of kissing Bea again from his mind.

Or try to, at least.

Chapter Seven

'Good to see you again, Rotherham!' The older and much shorter man rose at Griffin's entrance, his round face flushed, his riding jacket dark brown, the gaudily checked waistcoat beneath stretched to its limits over the portliness of his stomach, his brown Hessians dusty from his ride over to Stonehurst Park. 'You don't come to Stonehurst nearly enough!'

'Sir Walter.' Griffin nodded his cool acknowledgement of the other man. 'May I offer you some refreshment?' He chose to ignore Latham's comment regarding the frequency of his visits here; since Felicity died Griffin only came to Stonehurst perhaps once or twice a year, the memories of that disastrous marriage far too oppressive and immediate here, the place where Felicity had died.

'Thank you, but no.'

'Your visit into Yorkshire was successful, I hope?' He lowered his bulk down into one of the armchairs.

'Oh, my, yes.' The older man grinned as he resumed his seat opposite. 'I managed to buy myself a beautiful grey hunter.' He nodded his satisfaction.

Griffin nodded. 'Your butler informed me that Lady Francesca is away from home at the moment?'

'She was in London for part of the Season, acting as chaperone to my young niece. The two of them are presently making their way to Lancashire via several house parties.' The older man grimaced. 'I cannot abide London, or house parties, but for some reason Francesca enjoys all that social nonsense.'

Griffin smiled in sympathy; he too hated all that social nonsense, but had been forced to attend a certain amount of those functions when he was Felicity's husband. 'I am sure you will be pleased to have her and your niece returned to you.'

'Without a doubt,' Sir Walter agreed jovially. 'A house needs a woman's presence in it to feel anything like a home— Ah, but I apologise, Rotherham.' He frowned his consternation. 'That was in particularly bad taste, even for me.'

'Not at all,' Griffin dismissed dryly, having become accustomed to Sir Walter's bluntness over the years.

Besides which, Felicity's presence in any of his ducal homes had always made them feel less like a home to Griffin, and towards the end of their marriage that had been reason enough for him to wish to vacate those houses rather than suffer being in her frosty company a moment longer than was necessary.

A feeling in direct contrast to these past few days of ease he had shared living with Bea.

Damn it, he did not *live* with Bea, she was merely a guest in his home until such time as he could reunite her with her family.

And her lover.

'Although there is a rumour about the village

that you have brought a young lady here with you this time?' Sir Walter eyed him curiously.

Griffin had known that he could not keep Bea's presence here a secret for long, despite his previous threats to his household staff regarding gossip.

The rarity of Griffin's visits to Stonehurst was a cause for gossip in itself, and the village of Stonehurst was simply too parochial for it to escape the notice of the locals that a young lady had accompanied the Duke of Rotherham to Stonehurst Park. There was no doubt much speculation as to her identity.

'I believe you are referring to my god-daughter.' He nodded haughtily. 'Her parents have both recently died, and I have now taken guardianship of her.' Griffin felt no hesitation in enlarging upon the lie he had already perpetrated regarding the reason for Bea's presence here.

'She is but a child, then?'

'Not quite,' Griffin dismissed, having no idea of Bea's precise age, although he did not believe she could be any older than twenty.

The older man's eyes lit up with interest.

'Then no doubt Lady Francesca, once re-turned, will wish to invite you both over to dinner one evening while you are here, so that my niece and your goddaughter might become acquainted?'

'That will not be possible, I am afraid,' he refused smoothly. 'My goddaughter is still in mourning.'

'But surely a private dinner party is per-missible?'

'I am afraid not. Bea's emotions are still too delicate at present for us to give or receive social invitations. Another time, perhaps,' he dismissed briskly as he stood up and rang for Pelham in conclusion of the conversation.

'Of course.' Sir Walter rose to his feet as he took the hint it was time for him to leave. 'It really is good to see you back at Stonehurst Park again, Rotherham,' he added sincerely.

'Thank you.' Griffin nodded.

'You must at least ride over and see my new hunter when you have the time.'

'Perhaps,' Griffin replied noncommittally.

'No doubt the young ladies in the area are

also delighted at your return,' the older man added dryly.

Griffin did not dispute or agree with the statement as Pelham arrived to escort Sir Walter out, knowing it was his title the young ladies coveted. And he had learnt his lesson the hard way, in that regard!

'You did not return to the library earlier, once your guest had departed?' Bea prompted curiously as she and Griffin once again enjoyed a quiet dinner together in the small family dining room, Pelham having just left the room to go to the kitchen to collect their main course.

Griffin had been feeling too restless, too impatient with his current circumstances, to return to his work in the library.

And Bea.

Because he had realised, as he'd refused Sir Walter's dinner invitation on behalf of Bea as well as himself, that his protectiveness where Bea was concerned, his possessiveness towards her, the desire he felt for her, were growing deeper as each day passed.

And it was fast becoming an intolerable situation.

One that surely could not continue for much longer, without the danger of doing something he would sorely regret!

It certainly did not help that several more gowns had been delivered to Bea just yesterday, and that she wore one of those new gowns this evening.

Now that most of her visible bruises had faded, the pale peach colour of her new gown gave her face the appearance of warm and delectable cream, and her throat was a delicate arch, the bareness of her arms long and elegant. The darkness of her hair was swept up in a sophisticated cluster at her crown, with several loose wisps at her temples and nape.

She looked, in fact, every inch the beautiful and composed young lady of society that these past three days had convinced Griffin she truly must be.

A *unprotected* young lady of society, whom Griffin was finding it more and more difficult to resist taking in his arms and making love to!

'I do have other ducal responsibilities besides you, Bea,' he answered her with harsh dismissal. 'I cannot spend all of my time baby-sitting and mollycoddling you!'

'Of course.' It was impossible for Bea not to hear and inwardly flinch at the impatience in Griffin's tone. Or to feel hurt at being referred to as a responsibility. Even if that was what she so obviously meant to him.

It had been very silly of her to allow herself to grow so comfortable in Griffin's company these past few days. So comfortable, in fact, she had hoped that their time together might continue indefinitely.

Griffin was a duke, and, more importantly, he was a very handsome and eligible one. Her presence here, her unknown origins, must also be curtailing his own movements. Was it so surprising he did not wish to be burdened in-definitely with the responsibility of a young woman he did not even know, and, moreover, one who might very well turn out to be any-thing, from a thief to a murderess!

Bea carefully placed her napkin on the table beside her plate before standing up. 'I hope you will excuse me. I believe I have eaten enough for tonight.'

Griffin looked at her through narrowed lids as he stood up slowly, easily noting the pallor of her cheeks. 'You are unwell?'

'Not in the least.' Her chin rose. 'I am merely feeling a little fatigued.'

Griffin sighed at the distance he heard in her tone. 'I did not mean to be harsh with you just now.'

'You were not in the least harsh,' she assured him with that continued coolness. 'My presence here *is* a responsibility for you. And moreover it is one you did not wish or ask for.'

'Bea...'

'Please do not say any more just now, Griffin.' Tears glistened in her eyes as she looked up at him. 'Please allow me some dignity.' Bea turned and fled the room rather than finishing the sentence.

Griffin was once again left standing alone in a room after Bea had fled it in tears. And feeling just as impotent as to know what to do as he had the last time. As he had done in the past on those occasions when Felicity had chosen to remove herself from his company after he had said or done something she did not like. Admittedly she had rarely been in tears, but always with an air of coldness that had told him quite clearly she could no longer tolerate his company.

What was a man expected to do in such circumstances as these?

Bea was not his wife, nor was she related to him in any way, but for the moment she was his ward, and those tears glistening in her eyes indicated that, even if she was not crying, she was at the least very upset.

Should he follow Bea, and once again offer his apologies for his harshness? Or should he leave her to the solitude she was so obviously in need of?

He had respected Bea's need for solitude last time. Just as in the past Griffin had always respected Felicity's obvious aversion to his company, and his apologies for having offended her in some inexplicable way, by choosing not to intrude upon her solitude. But Bea was nothing like Felicity, and furthermore Griffin was well aware that it was he who was now responsible for her upset.

Bea was, without a doubt, a woman of great strength and fortitude, as she had demonstrated by her survival of her captivity and beatings, followed by her eventual escape. But even she must have her breaking points, and it appeared that Griffin's ill temper was one of them.

No doubt because he had become the only true stability in her world at present.

Griffin did not fool himself into thinking Bea felt any more for him than that. She was totally dependent upon him for everything, including the clothes she wore. At present, he was the only thing standing between her and the people who had abducted her. The same people who were no doubt searching for her even now. Unaware of her amnesia, they would hope to recapture her before she was able to tell anyone what had happened to her.

No matter that Griffin had been motivated by a sense of self-preservation just now, a defence against his increasing desire for Bea, he should not have been so short with her.

And whether she wished to see him again this evening or not, he *did* owe her an apology.

Bea was very aware that she had overreacted to Griffin's comment just now. That she was being unreasonable in expecting him to be in the least bit happy with their living arrangements. As no doubt Sir Walter Latham's visit earlier today had only emphasised.

Griffin had hardly left the four walls of Stonehurst Park these past three days, and usually only to go to the stables, or to talk with his estate manager. And rather than being able to relax and enjoy Sir Walter's visit earlier today, he had likely been forced to be restrained in his manner and to keep the visit short for fear a misspoken word might reveal Bea's presence here.

Whatever her own feelings of hurt just now she had behaved unreasonably by leaving the dinner table so abruptly, and she owed him an apology for possibly having caused him embarrassment when Pelham returned to the dining room and found her gone.

She drew in a deep steadying breath as she

fortified herself for going downstairs and facing Griffin again.

Only to come to an abrupt halt the moment she opened the door to her bedchamber and found Griffin standing outside in the hallway, his hand raised as if in preparation for knocking.

She gave a nervous smile. 'I was just coming downstairs to speak with you.'

'As I am here to speak to you.'

Bea stepped back in order to open the door wider. 'Please, come inside.'

Griffin stepped reluctantly into the bedchamber, aware that it was probably not wise. He noted how at home Bea had become in just a few days; there were combs and perfumes on the dressing table, the gown she had worn that day was draped over the chair, with a pair of matching satin slippers left on the floor beside it.

He turned back to Bea as she stood nervously in the centre of the bedchamber. 'I feel I owe you an apology and explanation for my behaviour earlier,' he began.

'I wish to apologise for having been so unreasonable earlier—'

Bea broke off as she realised that they had both begun to speak at the same time. And on the same subject. 'You have nothing to apologise for.' She gave a shake of her head. 'I am still somewhat emotional at the moment, and you have done so much for me already. My new gowns and slippers, the combs and perfumes.'

'I do not require your gratitude, Bea!' Griffin winced as he realised he had spoken harshly yet again. 'My impatience now, and earlier, is not with you, but due solely to frustration with this situation. I feel as if I should be doing more for you, not less, but until I receive word, or otherwise, from the friend I have contacted in London, my hands are tied.' He paced the bedchamber restlessly.

Bea knew of the letter he had sent to a well-connected acquaintance in London a few days ago. 'When do you expect to hear back from him?' The sooner he did, the sooner Bea might have the information she needed to remove herself from Stonehurst Park; she would no longer be a burden on Griffin's generosity.

She would be sad to leave here, and even sadder to leave Griffin, but had already accepted it was inevitable.

Griffin sighed. 'Perhaps in another three, possibly four days. I realise that is a lengthy time,' he acknowledged as Bea grimaced. 'But I do not see how I can expect to hear news any earlier than that when we are two hundred miles away from London. And there is always the possibility that there will be no news at all, or that Maystone may be away from home when my letter arrives,' he added grimly.

Bea accepted there might be delays that might occur in the delivery of Griffin's letter. Even if his friend did receive the missive, there was no guarantee that he would be able to garner any information about her. If that should be the case, she had no idea what she was going to do next. She could not remain with Griffin; that would be expecting too much, even from a man as generous as he. In which case, she had a week at most in which to formulate plans for her own future.

'You are not to worry about this, Bea.' Griffin frowned as he saw her look of concentration. 'There is no rush for you to leave here. You eat no more than a mouse, and are almost as quiet as one!'

A mouse?

Was that truly how Griffin regarded her? As a *mouse*?

Bea might have no memories of flirtation or society, but even so she was sure that being described as *a mouse* was not in the least complimentary. Or that she behaved in any way like one.

Griffin realised from Bea's dismayed expression that he had somehow spoken out of turn again, when he had meant only to reassure. The dealings between men and women really were as volatile to him as a powder keg; he had not felt this much out of his depth even with Felicity.

Perhaps that was because he actually cared what Bea thought of him? Whereas he had known that nothing he did or said was ever going to find approval from Felicity.

He frowned his impatience with the idea. 'That was not meant as an insult, Bea. Truth is, I have enjoyed the contented silence of your company these past few days,' he acknowledged grudgingly, never having believed he would ever say that to any woman.

Her face brightened. 'You have?'

Griffin once again acknowledged the danger of being alone with Bea in her bedchamber. Yet another habit he would have to break, if he was to continue behaving the gentleman.

Except his thoughts at this moment were far from gentlemanly!

He *had* enjoyed her company at the same time as he had been aware of everything about her. Bea's skin was so soft and creamy, her figure so womanly, her manner towards him so warm, and he had been too long without the warmth of any woman.

The logical part of his brain knew not to extend this dangerous situation any longer and that he should leave the bedchamber forthwith; while the part of his brain ruled completely by his desire told him to take what was in front of him, and to hell with the consequences!

Would Bea accept or reject him if he were to take her in his arms and kiss her again?

Would she accept him out of gratitude, for all that he had done and was still doing for her?

Griffin did not want any woman to accept his kisses out of gratitude.

Bea frowned at Griffin's continued silence. She believed that before her abduction she must have been a tactile person, a woman who liked to touch and be touched in return.

Because at this moment she wished for nothing more than to reach out and touch Griffin, to feel his arms close about her, to be crushed against the hardness of his chest and thighs, to lose herself in his strength and power, to feel *wanted*.

Was she imagining the hunger she saw burning in the depths of eyes? Was it possible he felt the same need for touch, for warmth, that she now did?

His wife had died six years ago but Bea did not deceive herself into believing a man as handsome as Griffin would not have occupied many women's beds in the years since.

Dared she hope, dream, that he now wished to occupy *her* bed, and it was only his sense of honour that was holding him back from doing so?

She moistened her slightly parted lips with the tip of her tongue. 'Griffin…'

'I have some estate work I need to complete this evening.' Griffin's expression was unreadable before he turned on his heel and walked to the closed door, his back towards her as he spoke again. 'I will instruct Pelham to bring you up a light supper tray. You did not eat nearly enough at dinner.'

'But, Griffin—'

'I wish you a good night, Bea,' he added firmly before opening the door and then closing it softly behind him as he left.

Bea felt the chill of disappointment at the abruptness of Griffin's departure. It was intolerable when she wanted, needed, *ached* to be close to him.

If Jacob Harker or his accomplice had violated her during her imprisonment then Bea had no memory of it—thank heavens. She shuddered. What she did know, with all certainty, was that her body had become attuned to Griffin's every move these past few days.

Her breasts swelled beneath her gown as she sat in the study with him, and a fire burned between her thighs whenever she watched him walk across the room, his movements unknowingly sensuous and graceful. She ached low in her belly whenever she imagined his large hands upon her own body, caressing, cupping, *stroking.*

She was sure she would have had these feeling towards Griffin no matter what the circumstances under which they had met.

Was she a wanton, to have such yearnings?

Could the warm feelings she now felt towards Griffin be so very wrong?

Her life was already in such turmoil, did she really want to add to that confusion by complicating things even further?

The answer to that question was *yes*!

It had become sheer torture for her to be so much in Griffin's company these past few days, and at the same time so aware of the barrier of formality he had erected between the two of them. To be aware of his deliberately avuncular attitude towards her.

A deliberation that had not been present in

those glittering eyes just minutes ago when Griffin had looked at her so hungrily.

Were her own feelings, her emotions, sure enough at present for her to know exactly what she would be doing if she were to meet the fire she believed she had seen in his gaze?

A mouse, he had called her, when in truth the only reason for Bea's quiet these past few days had been in the hopes of making her presence here more tolerable for him, to make herself less visible, so that she appeared less of a burden to him.

Whatever her station in life might have been before her amnesia, Bea knew with absolute certainty that she could not possibly have been *a mouse*. Griffin had also called her a woman of fortitude, and Bea did not doubt she was a woman of determination and resolve. Anything less and she would not have survived her abduction and the beatings, nor would she have managed to secure her own escape.

However, it was clear now that she would be gone from here soon, one way or another.

Away from Griffin.

She might never see him again!

She was not a mouse, and she would not have Griffin think of her as such, but was instead determined he would see the strong and capable woman she knew herself to be.

A woman who knew exactly who and what she wanted.

Chapter Eight

So much for his claim that he needed to work, Griffin acknowledged several hours later as he sat sprawled in the chair behind the desk in the library, a single lit candle on his desktop and the glow of the fire in the hearth to alleviate the darkness of the room behind him.

He had removed his jacket and cravat from earlier, several buttons of his shirt he'd also unfastened for added comfort, his thoughts ranging far and wide, before inevitably coming back to the exact same subject.

Bea.

His fingers clenched on the arms of his chair as he once again pictured her as she had looked in her bedchamber earlier: her hair slightly dishevelled, her cheeks flushed from the tears she had cried, her eyes dark with hurt, the swell of her breasts softly rising and falling as she breathed, her arms long and slender, hands and fingers delicately elegant. Hands he ached to have touch and stroke him.

She was desire incarnate!

A desire that was slowly but surely eating into Griffin's very soul, and driving him out of his mind.

'Griffin?'

Griffin turned so quickly in his chair at the unexpected sound of Bea's huskily soft voice, when he had been thinking of her so intensely, that he was in danger of falling out of it!

He almost did as he took in her appearance. She was framed in the doorway; her hair loose and silky about her shoulders, and she was wearing only her nightrail, with a thin silk robe over it and a matching belt fastened about the slenderness of her waist.

Griffin stood up, as was his custom when a lady entered the room, his brow lowering into a glower as he felt his body react instantly to Bea's appearance, and even more intensely than the uncomfortable and throbbing ache at dinner.

'What on earth are you still doing awake at this time of night?' His voice was husky as he tried to temper his tone, recalling how he had upset her when he had spoken to her harshly earlier.

She stepped into the room and closed the door quietly behind her before moving further into the shadowed library, the corners of the room completely dark. Only Griffin, his hair tousled, as if he had run his fingers through it several times in the past few hours, stood out in stark relief against that darkness. The unfastened shirt at his throat revealed a hint of dark hair covering his muscled chest.

Her chin rose determinedly before she lost her nerve and turned on her heel and fled. 'Has Pelham retired for the night?'

Griffin continued to glower. 'I believe so, yes.'

She nodded. 'I waited upstairs in my bedchamber after my bath until I believed he might have done,' she informed him softly.

His eyes narrowed warily. 'Why?'

Now that she was here, face to face with this physically mesmerising man, Bea was starting to wonder that herself!

It had all seemed so simple up in her bedchamber earlier. She would take a leisurely bath, wait for the household to go to bed before then going downstairs to seek out Griffin, with the intention of tempting him into kissing her again. With the intention of showing him she most certainly was not *a mouse*. Here and now, faced with the sheer masculinity of the man, she felt decidedly less confident.

What did she possibly have to offer a man of such sophistication and self-confidence as him? A man, a duke, who only had to snap his elegant fingers to have any woman he chose?

In her present loss of memory, homeless, friendless state, absolutely nothing.

Her nerve completely failed her. 'I have been afraid to fall asleep these past few nights because of the nightmares that occur when I do.' She drew in a deep and ragged breath.

Of course, Griffin acknowledged with a wince, he'd noticed these past few days, during their hours spent together in the library, that she occasionally dozed in her chair beside the fire. As if, he now realised, she had not slept at night.

'Would you like me to sit with you again until you have fallen asleep?' he suggested gruffly.

At the same time as he wondered if he was capable of being alone again with Bea in her bedchamber without making love with her. Or, more likely, once again suffering the tortures of hell as he tried to resist the urge to do so!

Her hair moved silkily against the soft swell of her breasts as she shook her head. 'I want—' She drew in a deep breath and began again. 'I should very much like it if you were to hold me in your arms again.'

He was doomed. His fate writ high in the heavens, as the man who had absolutely no defences when it came to the innocence of the very woman he was supposed to be protecting.

He cleared his throat before speaking. 'That would not be a good idea, Bea.'

She eyed him curiously. 'Why not?'

Griffin clenched his hands together behind his back. 'Please just accept that it would not.'

Bea studied him from beneath lowered dark lashes, easily noting the slightly fevered glitter in his eyes, and the flush high on those sharply etched cheekbones. There was a nerve pulsing in his tightly clenched jaw, and the width of his chest rapidly rose and fell as he breathed. 'I should like it very much if you did,' she insisted softly.

He eyed her impatiently. 'What are you doing?' he barked even as his hands came quickly from behind his back as she hurtled across the room and into his arms.

Her arms were about his waist as she burrowed into the comforting hardness of his chest. 'I feel so safe when you hold me in your arms, Griffin.'

Safe? Griffin echoed the word incredulously.

Bea felt *safe* when he held her?

It was the very *last* thing she was when his body reacted so viscerally to the feel of the warm softness of her body nestled so closely against it. He was a man of flesh and blood, not a blasted saint!

As the swell of his arousal testified.

Bea sighed her contentment. 'This is so very nice.'

His gaze sharpened with suspicion as she looked up at him. Was that a glint of mischief he could see in her eyes? A curve of womanly satisfaction to the fullness of her lips?

It was, damn it!

He pulled back slightly so that he could see her face more clearly; yes, he could definitely see challenge now in the darkness of her gaze, and her creamy cheeks were flushed. 'Bea, are you playing a game with me?'

'A game?'

Griffin wasn't fooled for a moment by her too-innocent expression. 'A dangerous game.' He nodded grimly.

'Dangerous?' she echoed softly, her fingertips playing lightly across his chest.

'Very dangerous,' he assured her firmly as his hands moved to grasp the tops of her arms to hold her firmly away from him. 'I advise that you leave here now, Bea, or suffer the consequences,' he warned.

Heat and caution waged war within Bea. The heat of the desire she felt for Griffin, to be closer to him. And the caution of realising that the man who now stood before her was not that same easy companion of the past few days. Or the gentleman who had pledged to protect her until her true protector could be found.

This Griffin was not a gentleman at all, but was instead pure, predatory male. A man who was rakishly handsome and wholly sensual, his gaze now feasting hungrily on the firm swell of her breasts visible above her nightrail and robe.

Perhaps she did have something to offer him, after all?

Bea moistened her lips with the tip of her tongue before she spoke slowly. 'I believe I will choose the consequences.'

'Then you are a reckless fool!' Griffin grated even as he pulled her into his arms and his mouth laid siege to hers.

Bea groaned her satisfaction as she gave herself up to the savagery of his kiss, eagerly standing on tiptoe as she moulded her body against his much harder one.

Her hands moved up his chest, feeling the soft hair visible there, lingering for several sec-onds, caressing that silkiness, as he moaned softly. She then slid her hands over the muscled width of his shoulders, her fingers becoming entangled in the darkness of the hair at his nape as the heat between them intensified and grew.

Bea whimpered low in her throat as Griffin now widened her stance to grind the hardness of his arousal into the inviting softness between her thighs, drawing her breath in sharply through her nose as he touched a part of her that caused the heated pleasure to course wildly through her veins.

She was lost in a maelstrom of emotions as his mouth continued to devour hers, even as his large hands restlessly caressed the length of her spine before settling on her bottom as he pulled Bea in even closer. The rhythmic stroking of his arousal now sent heated pleasure through the whole of her body; her nipples were full and aching, and between her thighs was swollen and warm.

Reckless fool or not, Bea didn't want Griffin to stop. She wanted this pleasure to go on and on. To lose herself utterly, in both Griffin's arms and his unmistakeable passion.

Griffin wanted all Bea had to give. His

hands cupped beneath the weight of her breasts and the soft pad of his thumbs caressed the swollen and sensitive tips. Bea's passion, Bea's pleasure, every inch of Bea's body.

Her kisses revealed the first, her groans, as he caressed her breasts showed the second, and the third—

Griffin pulled back abruptly to draw ragged breath into his starved lungs as he looked down at her with heated eyes. 'You should go back to your bedchamber, Bea. Now!'

Her hair was tousled, her eyes heavy with passion, cheeks flushed and feverish, her lips swollen from their kisses. 'I would rather stay here, with you.'

'It will very shortly be too late for me to stop, Bea.'

She looked up at him searchingly. 'Do you want to stop?'

What he wanted was this woman's body spread naked before him, so that he could kiss and taste every inch of her, from her head to her toes!

He clenched his jaw. 'No, I do not want to stop.'

'Then neither do I,' she assured him gently, her gaze continuing to hold his as her fingers moved purposefully to unfasten the two remaining buttons of his shirt.

His breath caught in his throat as she pulled his shirt free of his pantaloons before sliding it slowly up his chest. 'You really are playing with fire, Bea,' he gave her one last, growled warning.

She smiled up at him impishly. 'Then at least I shall be kept warm!' She pulled his shirt up, removing it completely. Her eyes were hot and devouring as she gazed at the muscled bareness of his chest before tentatively touching. 'You truly are magnificent, Griffin!' she breathed wonderingly as she smoothed her hands across his chest and over his nipples.

Her words, and her touch, caused Griffin's desire for her to rage out of control.

He had no memory of when a woman had last desired him for himself, and not because of his title or because she was being paid to want him. A sad state of affairs, indeed, but he had felt too raw after Felicity—

No!

He would not think of Felicity now.

Why should he think of her when there had been such an impenetrable coldness to his wife? A coolness he already knew Bea did not share.

Bea was warm—so very warm. She was responsive. Even now the hard berries of her nipples throbbed heatedly against the soft pads of his thumbs. And the scent of her arousal teased and tempted his senses, a mixture of honey and earthy, desirable woman.

Perhaps he should spare a thought for the man Michael, the man she had called for in her sleep.

Griffin saw no reason why he should consider him when Bea seemed bound and determined not to!

'Are you sure this is what you really want?' Griffin knew *he* was the one who had to be sure; he had to know that Bea wanted him as much as he desired to make love to her.

'Very sure,' she answered without hesitation.

He gave her one last searching glance, seeing only sincerity in her expression, before taking her hand and drawing her over to the warmth of the fireplace. He came to a halt and turned to face her, his gaze deliberately holding hers as he unfastened the robe at her waist before slipping it from her shoulders and allowing it to drop onto the rug on which they both stood.

She wore only her nightrail now, a diaphanous garment easily penetrated by the flickering firelight, and revealing every dip and curve of Bea's body as Griffin gazed down at her hungrily. Her breasts were full and tipped by ruby red and swollen berries, her waist slender above the womanly flare of her hips. Dark curls nestled temptingly between her thighs, and her legs were smooth and shapely above slender bare feet.

Bea sensed that Griffin hesitated still, not because he did not want her—the evidence of that was all too apparent in the tenting of his pantaloons—but because he was, after all, a gentleman, even in his desire for her.

How lucky his wife had been to have such a considerate husband. To have such a wonderful man in love with her. To be so privileged as to possess the care and devotion of such a man.

The desire Griffin now felt for her might only be a shadow of the emotions he had once felt for his dead wife, but surely it was enough?

Bea would make it be enough!

She continued to look into his eyes rather than down at her own body as her hands moved down to take hold of her nightgown. She slowly drew the material up to reveal her calves, then her thighs. The blush deepened in her cheeks as she raised the garment to her waist and saw Griffin's eyes darken, his heated gaze fixed on the V of silky ebony curls between her thighs.

'Higher,' he encouraged tightly.

Bea's hands trembled as she slowly pulled her nightrail up over her waist and breasts, her legs starting to shake as she heard his harshly indrawn breath as she removed the garment completely, dropping it down beside her robe as she stood naked before him.

'How beautiful you are,' he murmured as he sank to his knees in front of her, his large hands cupping both her breasts as he drank in his fill before slowly leaning forward to suckle one of her aching and engorged nipples into the moist heat of his mouth.

Bea reached out to grasp his bared shoulders as sharp pleasure engulfed her. She was afraid her legs would no longer support her if she didn't. His chest was bathed in firelight, warm and dry beneath her fingers, and she could feel the play of muscles beneath his skin as Griffin caressed her.

Bea had never dreamt that such pleasure existed as that created by the complete intimacy of having Griffin on his knees before her, his bared flesh beneath her caressing fingertips, her aching nipple in his mouth.

The pleasure intensified as he now drew hungrily on her swollen berry, the fingers and thumb of his other hand stroking and squeezing its twin, and sending waves of heated pleasure coursing through Bea's body straight down to between her thighs.

Soft moans began to penetrate the silence of the room, and Bea realised they were her own as one of her hands moved to clasp the back of Griffin's head, her fingers becoming entangled in the dark thickness of his hair as she held him to her, never ever wanting this pleasure to stop.

Wanting *more*.

But having no idea what more there was.

Griffin looked up at Bea as he felt her restlessness; her eyes were closed, long lashes resting on flushed cheeks, her lips parted slightly as she breathed raggedly, her throat arched in pleasure as she thrust her breasts forward.

He lightly caressed her waist as he slowly released her nipple from his mouth.

'Griffin!' She looked down at him, need shining brightly in the feverish glow of eyes.

He took a few seconds to enjoy the sight of her engorged nipple, so moist and red and swollen from his suckling, before his gaze moved lower, his hands now resting on her hips as he held her in place before him and gently nudged her legs apart with his knees.

She was so aroused. For him. Because of him. Because of her desire for him.

'Griffin?' Bea's voice quivered her uncertainty as she watched his long fingers gently part the ebony curls between her thighs before he once again lowered his head towards her.

He glanced up at her, so close now the warmth of his breath brushed softly against a part of her that felt swollen and aching. 'Do you trust me, Bea?' he prompted huskily.

'Of course I trust you.' If she did not trust Griffin, then she could never, would never, trust anyone again.

'Then trust me now.' He blew delicately against that swollen ache between her thighs, causing her to shudder and tremble with the pleasure of that caress. 'Do you like that?'

'Yes,' she groaned weakly, fingers now digging painfully into his muscled shoulders. Although Griffin seemed unaware of any pain.

'And this?' He slowly lathed the rough length of his tongue against her swollen flesh.

'Yes!' Bea's cheeks suffused with embarrassed colour at the intimacy even as she rose up on tiptoe as the force of that pleasurable caress ripped through the whole of her body.

He moved back slightly before taking her hand and tugging lightly until she sat down on the rug beside him. 'I will not hurt you, Bea,' he assured her gruffly. 'I will never do anything to hurt you or endanger you.' He cupped her face in his hands before his lips gently claimed hers.

Bea was so befuddled by the end of that long and satisfying kiss that she offered no further hesitation as Griffin pushed her gently down onto the rug before parting her legs and settling the width of his shoulders between them.

She groaned low in her throat at the first touch of his tongue against that swollen ache between her thighs. Her hands fell limply to her sides, eyes closing as she became lost in the pleasure of that moist and rhythmic caress. A pressure began to build inside her that she did not understand. Did not need to understand. She needed only to *feel*, as Griffin's hands cupped the cheeks of her bottom to tilt her up to him, like a sacrifice on an altar.

'Griffin!' She gasped as the pressure built and built. Until it grew so high, so intense, she felt as if her whole body might explode from the joy of it.

Until she did explode, deep inside her, the intense pleasure radiating outwards as well as inwards until she lay weak and gasping.

'Wh—what was that?' she gasped weakly.

Griffin moved to lie beside her as he slowly licked her juices from his lips. 'The French call it *le petit mort*—the little death,' he translated huskily.

Bea certainly felt as if she had died and gone to heaven and she was sure that she had never experienced pleasure like it.

'The English refer to it as a climax, or an orgasm.' Griffin smoothed the hair back from the dampness of her brow.

'I— Does that—does that always happen to a woman when—when a man and woman are t-together?' she prompted shyly.

'Only if the man cares enough to ensure her pleasure, which sadly too many rarely do.' His jaw tightened. 'And if the woman allows herself to become excited or stimulated.'

Bea gazed up at him searchingly, detecting a bitterness beneath his tone and the sudden bleakness of his expression. She was too satiated, too lethargic to care at that moment as she lay unabashedly naked beside him. Modesty seemed a little silly when Griffin had not only looked at her most intimate of places, but had also licked and tasted her there.

All bitterness fled as he smiled down at her,

his gaze warm. 'You are a singular woman, Bea. Very passionate and giving.'

She smiled. 'I believe *you* are the one who is remarkable, for having ignited that passion. I— Does a man experience that same climax?'

Griffin drew in a sharp breath, unsure of how to answer her. It was obvious Bea was an innocent, that her own responses just now had surprised her, her orgasm was a shock to her. How much more shocked would she be if she were to see him achieve his climax?

'Griffin?'

He closed his eyes briefly before looking at her. 'I do not know how to answer you, Bea,' he admitted honestly.

'With the truth?'

Griffin's lids lowered. 'My own arousal is more physically visible than your own.'

'The swelling in your pantaloons?'

'The swelling in my pantaloons,' he confirmed uncomfortably.

She sat up slightly. 'Would you—? Can I see it?'

He swallowed as he saw how pretty her breasts looked as she sat forward, so firm and uptilting, her nipples still swollen and rouged from his earlier ministrations.

He gave a shake of his head. 'That would not be a good idea.' Felicity had visibly paled the first time she had seen him naked. Despite all his efforts to arouse her, to ease his passage, she had screamed the first time he had penetrated her, until he had retreated again when her sobs had become too much for him to bear. The second time had been no better, nor the third, thus setting a pattern for their physical intimacy that had never changed.

Not that he intended to penetrate Bea. She was an unmarried lady, an innocent still, whether she believed it or not, and once inside her Griffin knew he would be unable to stop himself from spilling his seed.

No, far better that he should send Bea back to her bed before he returned to his own chamber, where he could douse himself in cold water! 'I believe you might sleep now if you were to return to your bedchamber.'

Bea was sure that she would, her body having an unaccustomed lethargy, a feeling of fullness and satiation, and no doubt resulting from her orgasm.

But she did not feel like falling asleep. She did not want their time together to be over just yet, and there was still that intriguing bulge in Griffin's pantaloons to explore.

'May I please see?' She looked at him encouragingly.

His jaw tightened as he obviously waged his own inner battle. Quite what that battle was, Bea had no idea, but she knew that there was one from the stormy grey of his eyes and the clenching of his jaw.

'You really are a witch!' He groaned his defeat and began to unfasten his pantaloons. 'The moment you are frightened you will tell me to stop.'

'Frightened?' Bea looked at him incredulously as she watched that unfastening in fascination. 'Why would I be frightened?'

'You are a genteel lady and I am...overlarge, in that area,' he acknowledged reluctantly as he unfastened the tie of his drawers.

'But that is surely because you are altogether an overlarge man?'

'Yes,' he bit out grimly. 'But some ladies find me unpleasantly so. Especially here.' He folded back his drawers as he spoke the last word, allowing his arousal to spring free of all restraint as he lay back on the rug and stared up at the shadowed ceiling.

Almost as if he could not physically bear to watch her reaction, Bea realised.

She sat up completely, her fascinated gaze fixed on his member; surrounded by dark curls at its base, it was indeed an impressive size, but Bea saw no reason at all for fear. She looked up at Griffin's face, frowning as she saw how pale and strained he looked. 'Does it hurt to be so swollen?'

'No.' His voice sounded strange, strangulated.

'Then may I touch it?'

'Bea...' He broke off his angry outburst as she flinched back, his eyes glittering darkly. 'If you touch me I am afraid I shall—I shall be unable to maintain control myself!' he bit out forcefully.

'You will climax?'

'Without a doubt I shall, yes!'

Bea gave a confused shake of her head. 'Why should you not, when I have already done so?' Her cheeks felt warm.

Griffin drew in a deep and controlling breath. 'You asked to see and I have shown you. Are you not fearful? Overwhelmed by my size?'

'If I am overwhelmed then it is at your magnificence,' she assured him softly. 'And, no, I am not in the least frightened. Why should I be when this is a part of you?' She touched him gently with her fingertips, incredulous at how soft his skin felt when he was obviously so fiercely hard.

He was steel encased in warm velvet, her touches becoming bolder still as Griffin made no further objection to her explorations, although the grinding of his teeth spoke of his inner fight to remain in control as her hand cupped him.

He drew his breath in sharply as Bea's other hand then moved to close about him, and, recalling how Griffin had made love to her, she began to lower her head with the intention of feeling him with her mouth, her tongue.

'No, Bea!' Griffin groaned weakly in protest even as his body burned for more of her touch.

'Will it hurt you if I do?'

'No. But— *Saints protect me!*' He groaned as her tongue tentatively licked his length.

Griffin groaned his pleasure as she licked and tasted, causing Bea's fingers to tighten as she began to stroke until he began to thrust up into her encircling fingers. She reacted instinctively as she widened her lips and took him into the heat of her mouth.

'You are killing me, Bea!' Griffin gasped weakly, hands reaching out to grasp her shoulders.

Bea did not believe that for a moment, knew from the throb and heat of him in her hands, and the fact that he was holding her closer rather than pushing her away, that Griffin would shortly experience that same intense pleasure as she had just minutes ago.

The *petit mort*.

The little death of pleasure.

And she wanted to give this to him. Wanted to *share* this with him.

She had no idea why any other ladies should

ever have been frightened of him. Why he should have been so reluctant to let her see and touch him, when his body was so truly magnificent. Nor did she care. At this moment, here and now, there was only herself and Griffin.

Heat engulfed her own body for a second time at the sounds of Griffin's groans of pleasure.

'Stop now, Bea! For goodness' sake, you have to stop…' Griffin's protest turned to a loud and aching groan as his own pleasure overtook his control, his fingers digging painfully into her shoulders as he continued to gasp his pleasure.

The arousal of Bea's own body rose with each hot and pulsing jet of Griffin's release, heat engulfing her as she climaxed for a second time, adding her own groans of completion to Griffin's.

Chapter Nine

Griffin was at a loss as to know what to do next, his fingers lightly stroking the dark silkiness of Bea's hair as she lay with her head against the dampness of his thighs, his body now totally spent.

As he now felt totally relaxed and at ease in Bea's company.

Had he ever felt such a connection to any woman?

Had any other woman ever given to him so wholeheartedly as Bea just had?

Had any other woman climaxed just from giving him pleasure, as he knew Bea had?

Never, came the instant answer to all those questions.

But what to do now?

The complications of what they had just done together weighed heavily on Griffin's shoulders. He did not need to offer marriage, of course. Precarious as Bea's life seemed at the moment, she did not need to add to that uncertainty by taking such a socially inept man as her husband!

But should he at least insist she return to her own bedchamber before going to his?

Would she be happy with that, or would she want him to stay with her tonight?

Just thinking of lying beside her for the whole night, his body wrapped protectively about hers, was enough to cause his body to throb in anticipation of further lovemaking.

Lovemaking that should not—could not—happen again.

Tonight they had given each other pleasure with their mouths and hands, but if it was allowed to happen again how long before they—*he*—wanted more? Before he wished to possess Bea totally? How long before making love put them both at risk, so that marriage was no longer an option but a certainty?

Bea was warm and giving, yes, but Griffin

did not need her to say the words to know that she would not want to tie herself to a man such as him for ever because of an unborn child.

Especially so when somewhere a man called Michael was awaiting her return.

'You are very quiet,' Bea said as she raised her head to look at him.

Griffin breathed in deeply before speaking. 'I was just thinking that—' He paused with a frown as there came the sound of a loud knocking. 'What the devil?' He sat up abruptly, a scowl marring his brow as he turned towards the door.

Bea also frowned at the interruption; she was desperate to know what Griffin had been thinking as he'd lain so quiet and unmoving beneath her.

Was he as happy as she was, overwhelmed by the warmth of emotions flowing between them?

Or was he regretting what had just happened between the two of them, and seeking some way in which to gently but firmly express those regrets?

'You must dress immediately,' he instructed

harshly as there came the sound of another loud
pounding, causing him to rise quickly to his
feet before hastily fastening his pantaloons.
'Now, Bea.' He scowled darkly as she still sat
naked upon the hearthrug. 'It would seem we
have a visitor, and you cannot be seen like
this!' He gathered up her nightrail and robe
and pushed them into her trembling hands.
'Make haste, Bea,' he encouraged impatiently
as he pulled his shirt on over his head before
turning away.

Bea felt bereft as she watched Griffin march
across the room to the door and leave the library without sparing her so much as a second glance.

As if he had already forgotten the intimacies
the two of them had just shared.

And perhaps he had. Perhaps men did not
feel the same way about such things? Did they
not appreciate the vulnerability that occurred
inside a woman when she placed her trust, her
naked self, so completely into the hands of another human being?

Certainly Griffin would not have been cel-
ibate in the years since his wife's death and

yet he remained unencumbered by a second marriage, which would seem to imply that his affections had never been engaged in any of those liaisons.

Had Bea been foolish to believe that she was somehow different from the other women he had made love to, and that Griffin held some measure of affection for her?

Or was it just, in her determination to show Griffin she was not the mouse he believed her to be as well as her need to be with him, that she had deliberately chosen to *believe* that he cared for her?

Her memories of her own past might be seriously lacking at present, but still she knew instinctively that men were different from women, in that their physical desires were not necessarily accompanied by the same feelings of affection or love.

Love?

Did she *love* Griffin?

She certainly cared for him a good deal, and would be very sad to part from him when the time came, but was that love?

'Perhaps now that I have persuaded Pelham

to go back to bed you will explain what the hell you are doing here!' she heard Griffin hiss fiercely from outside in the hallway.

'I would rather we were alone together in a private room before doing that,' a male voice replied unconcernedly. 'With the door closed so that we cannot be overheard— Hello, who have we here?'

Bea viewed the newcomer nervously as he stepped inside the library, one blond eyebrow raised in mocking query as he slowly took in her appearance from the top of her head to her toes.

Lavender eyes.

The man had lavender-coloured eyes, Bea realised inconsequentially.

Bright, wickedly sparkling eyes, set in a face of such aristocratic handsomeness that he was likely to take a woman's breath away at a glance.

His eyes were fringed by thick dark lashes, his nose was perfectly straight between high pronounced cheekbones, chiselled lips curved into a speculative smile above a surprisingly determined jaw.

As tall as Griffin, and almost as broad across the shoulders, the blond-haired gentleman was dressed in the height of fashion, despite the lateness of the hour. His superfine was a perfectly tailored black, his linen snowy white, a diamond pin nestled in the folds of his neckcloth. He had a tapered waist and hips, long legs, the layer of dust on his black boots the only evidence that he had almost certainly arrived here on horseback.

He turned his quizzical gaze on his host. 'Griff?'

'Bea, this is my friend Christian Seaton, the Duke of Sutherland,' Griffin introduced tersely.

The thing he had dreaded when he'd sent that letter to Maystone, that one of the Dangerous Dukes would hasten to Lancashire, had indeed come to pass. The question was, how much had Maystone imparted regarding the situation here?

He and Christian had a long-standing affection for each other, having attended Eton together, along with the other Dangerous Dukes, but even so Griffin knew that Christian was everything that he was not. Elegant. Charming. Fashionably dressed, no matter what the occasion.

Women had been known to swoon at Christian. Sensible women, matronly women, as well as the twittering debutantes who appeared in society every Season.

And Bea, Griffin noted somewhat sourly, had been unable to take her eyes off the man since he'd appeared in the doorway!

Was that *jealousy* Griffin felt towards his friend's easy charm and good looks?

Ridiculous.

And yet those feelings of bad humour persisted as he finished the introduction. 'Christian, this is my goddaughter, Beatrix.'

Bea offered Christian a shy smile. 'I prefer to be called Bea, Your Grace,' she invited huskily.

'I am pleased to meet you, Bea.' Christian nodded before turning to look at Griffin with narrowed, mocking eyes. 'Your goddaughter, Griff? Was that the best you could come up with?'

Griffin scowled darkly. 'The situation is not what you have assumed it to be.'

'Maystone has made me fully aware of what the situation is, Griff,' Christian assured him as he strolled further into the room to take Bea's hand in his before raising it to his lips. 'I trust you are now recovered somewhat from your unpleasant ordeal?'

Griffin's mouth tightened as he realised that Christian did indeed know exactly how Bea had come to be a guest at Stonehurst Park. Just as he could see, by the sudden wariness in Bea's expression, she was also aware of Sutherland's insight into the reason for her presence here.

'Maystone sent you?' Griffin queried abruptly.

Christian finally released Bea's hand as he turned to Griffin.

'Maystone is also on his way here. By carriage. I was able to travel faster on horseback.'

Griffin had not expected his letter of query to Maystone to have elicited quite such a reaction as this. It did not bode well regarding the outcome of that query.

'I am to assist in protecting your...goddaughter until Maystone arrives and explains all,' Christian added grimly.

Bea was uncomfortable at learning that the Duke of Sutherland seemed aware of the details of her current situation. Most especially so because she had never heard of the gentleman until his arrival a few minutes ago. 'Griffin?' she asked uncertainly.

Griffin moved to stand at her side. 'Christian is a trusted friend, Bea,' he assured her gruffly.

That might well be true. But was it not humiliating enough that Griffin knew of her circumstances, without the charmingly handsome Duke of Sutherland being aware of them too?

She turned to look at the man now. 'Do you know my true identity, sir?'

'I do,' he confirmed abruptly.

'And?' she prompted as he added nothing to that statement.

He winced. 'I have been instructed not to discuss the matter until Lord Maystone arrives.'

Bea stared at him incredulously. 'That is utterly ridiculous. Surely I have a right to know

who I am? Why those things were done to me?'
Two bright spots of angry colour burned in her
cheeks as she glared at Christian Seaton.

'You have every right, yes.' He sighed. 'Unfortunately, I am not presently at liberty to discuss it.'

'Griffin?' Bea turned her angry gaze on
him.

Griffin was as much at a loss as Bea. Except
to know that Christian's silence on the subject, his added protection, implied Bea's situation was even graver than he had anticipated it
might be. 'I believe that, for the moment, Bea,
we will have to accept Sutherland's reticence
on the subject.' His gaze remained on Christian as he answered Bea, knowing by the other
man's expression that he was not remaining silent out of playfulness but necessity.

'By "we" I am to presume you mean me.'
She glared. 'For no doubt the two of *you* will
discuss the matter at your earliest conve-
nience!'

Griffin winced. 'Perhaps it is time you returned to bed, Bea?'

'I shall do no such thing!' she said angrily.

'I am not a child to be ordered to my room. This man—this *Duke*—knows exactly who I am, and yet says he is not at liberty to reveal it. And you *agree* with him!' She glared at Griffin incredulously.

As Bea had no knowledge of the work he and Christian had been involved in for the Crown for so many years, she could not possibly understand the need there often was for secrecy, even from each other. 'Christian must have his reasons.'

'None that are acceptable to me, I assure you!' She was breathing hard in her agitation, and with each breath Griffin was able to make out the hard, aroused pebbles of her nipples against her robe.

Which meant that Christian must be able to see that delectable display too.

Griffin's jaw tightened. 'I really think it best if you return to your bedchamber now, Bea.'

'And I have said that I have no wish to return to my bedchamber!'

'The two of us will talk again in the morning,' Griffin concluded firmly.

Bea glared first at Griffin and then at Sutherland, and back to Griffin. 'You are both mad if you believe I will calmly accept this silence until this Lord Maystone arrives!' She gathered up the bottom of her robe with an angry swish. 'I will give you both until morning to discuss the matter, and then I shall *demand* to know the answers!' She turned on her heel and marched angrily from the room.

'What a fascinating young woman,' Christian breathed as he gazed after her admiringly.

'You will keep your lethal charms to yourself where Bea is concerned.' Griffin was in no mood at present—or any other time, he suspected—to listen to or behold another man's admiration for Bea.

Christian gave him a long and considering stare. 'As you wish,' he finally drawled softly. 'In the meantime, perhaps you might care to explain to me just exactly what it was you were doing in the library with your "goddaughter" at this time of the night?'

Griffin felt his face go pale.

Hateful.

Hateful *and* impossible, Bea decided as she

angrily paced the length and breadth of her bedchamber.

Both of them!

How *could* Griffin, especially after the intimacies they had so recently shared, possibly side with the hateful Duke of Sutherland?

Why was her identity such a secret?

Who was she, and what had she done, that Christian Seaton refused to discuss it in front of her?

Bea sank down on the side of her bed, weariness overtaking her as the events of the evening finally took their toll on her.

Just a short time ago she had been so happy, had felt so utterly desired, so satiated in that desire, yet now it was as if that closeness between herself and Griffin had never taken place. As if there was a distance between them so wide it might never be bridged.

Her cheeks heated as she thought of the intimacies they had shared. The pleasure Griffin had given her with both his hands and mouth. The unmistakeable pleasure she had given him in return. The taste of him on her lips.

Oh, dear Lord, would Seaton *know* that the

two of them had been making love shortly before his arrival?

Griffin's appearance had certainly been dishevelled enough; he had not bothered to resume wearing his neckcloth or waistcoat and jacket before striding out into the hallway, and his hair was in disarray from her caressing fingers. Just as his lips had looked as puffy and swollen as her own now felt.

Would Christian Seaton, wickedly handsome, and so obviously a sophisticated gentleman of the world, have been able to tell, just from looking at the two of them, that she and Griffin had been making love together when he arrived?

Oh, dear Lord, could this night become any more humiliating?

Bea gave a muffled sob as she buried her face in the pillow, once again afraid. Of the knowledge of her past. Of what her future might hold.

Of having to leave Griffin.

'I would not care to discuss it, no,' Griffin answered the other man tightly as he moved to lift the decanter on his desk, pouring brandy into two of the crystal glasses before handing one to his friend. 'Who is she, Christian? And why all the secrecy?'

Christian took a grateful swallow of the amber liquid before answering him. 'We believe her name to be Lady Beatrix Stanton. She is nineteen years of age, and the unmarried daughter of the Earl and Countess of Barnstable. You will recall that both the Earl and his countess perished in a carriage accident last year? As for the rest...' He grimaced. 'The demand for secrecy is all Maystone's doing, I am afraid.'

Bea's name was Beatrix Stanton. She was the unmarried *Lady* Beatrix Stanton, Griffin corrected grimly, relieved at the former and satisfied that his previous conviction that Bea was a lady was a true one.

He had known her father, damn it; the two of them had belonged to the same club in London. Unfortunately Griffin had been out of the country when Barnstable and his countess had died so he had been unable to attend the funeral.

But he had known Bea's father!

Griffin threw some of the brandy to the back of his own throat, face grim as his thoughts raced.

Bea's dream of having attended her parents' funeral had been a true one.

So, then, must be the dream of her abduction, imprisonment, and the beatings.

Not that Griffin had ever had any doubts regarding the latter even if he did not know the reason for it.

And what of the man, Michael? He then must also be real.

Exactly who was he, and what did he mean to Bea?

He looked sharply across at Sutherland as the other man now slouched down in one of the chairs before the fire, no doubt tired from the strains of his hurried journey. 'If her parents are both dead, then who is now her guardian?'

The other man looked up at him beneath hooded lids. 'Apart from having you as her godfather, you mean?'

'Christian—'

'I am sorry, Griff, but I believe you are now

crossing into the area where Maystone has demanded secrecy.' Sutherland grimaced.

Griffin's eyes widened. 'You are refusing to tell me who Bea's guardian is?'

The other man's mouth tightened. 'I am ordered not to tell you, Griff. There is a difference. This does not just involve the young lady you have claimed as your goddaughter,' he bit out harshly as Griffin looked set to explode into anger. 'The lives of other innocents are also at stake.'

Griffin stilled, eyes narrowed. 'What others?' he demanded. 'I always could pummel you into the ground, Christian,' he reminded grimly as the other man sipped his brandy rather than answer his question.

Sutherland sighed heavily as he relaxed back in the chair. 'Then you will just have to pummel away, I am afraid, Griffin, because I am not—'

'You are not at liberty to tell me,' Griffin finished grimly. 'Maystone believes Bea's life is still in danger?' he added sharply.

'It is the reason I have travelled here so quickly,' Christian confirmed.

Part of Griffin bristled at Maystone having doubted that he alone could protect Bea. Another part of him was grateful to have Christian's assistance.

If Bea truly was still in danger, then he welcomed any assistance in ensuring her safety.

He sighed heavily. 'How long before Maystone arrives, do you estimate?'

'Another day at best, possibly two, or even three at worst.'

Griffin inwardly chafed at the delay. 'And in the meantime?'

'In the meantime we do not let your young ward out of our sight. And, Griffin?'

'Yes?' He answered warily; he might welcome Christian's help in keeping Bea safe, but he was not altogether happy with the thought of the other man keeping such a close watch over Bea.

'Have a care where she is concerned, will you?' Christian suggested gently.

His shoulders tensed. 'I would not harm a hair upon her head!'

'I was thinking more of your own welfare than of hers.'

Griffin's eyes narrowed. 'I am only concerned for Bea, for the harsh treatment she has suffered, and the reason behind it. Nothing more.'

'I know you, Griffin.' Christian sighed. 'On the outside you are harsh and gruff, keeping the world and others at a distance, but on the inside—'

'On the inside I am just as harsh and gruff,' Griff assured him with some of that harshness. 'And whatever you may think you witnessed here this evening, let me assure you that you are mistaken if you believe that either my own or Bea's emotions were seriously engaged. It was…a mistake, an impulse, of the moment. She was upset, I attempted to comfort her, and the situation spiralled out of control. It will not happen again.'

'No?'

'No!' Even as he had made the explanation, and now the denial, Griffin knew that he was not being altogether truthful. With himself or Christian.

He *had* been attempting to comfort Bea earlier, but she had made it clear that she needed something else from him, something more.

Something he had been only too willing to give her.

And would willingly give time and time again if asked.

Bea, listening outside the study door, having cried her tears and decided to return down the stairs with the intention of demanding that Seaton give her the answers to her many questions, instead now felt as if her heart were breaking hearing Griffin describe their lovemaking as a mistake that he would not allow to happen again...

Chapter Ten

'You must try to eat something more than toast, Bea,' Griffin encouraged as they sat at the breakfast table the following morning, where she only nibbled at a dry piece of toast and took the occasional sip of her tea.

Griffin had been unsure of what Bea's mood would be today, after their…closeness the previous evening, and followed by Christian's unexpected arrival, and Bea's own heated departure from the room.

After her threats he had certainly not expected her uncharacteristic silence this morning, other than when she replied with stilted politeness to whatever remark he or Christian addressed to her directly.

'Thank you, but I am not hungry,' she answered him in just that manner now.

'Did you have more nightmares last night?' Griffin asked with concern, having noted the pallor of Bea's face the minute she'd entered the breakfast room, where he and Christian were already seated and enjoying breakfast. Her pallor did not in any way, though, detract from her fresh beauty, dressed as she was today in a pretty yellow gown that complemented her creamy complexion and gave an ebony richness to her hair.

Bea looked coolly across the table at him. 'How am I to tell, when my life has become nothing but a continuous nightmare from which I would rather awaken?'

Griffin scowled as he saw the corners of Christian's lips twitch with amusement as the other man obviously heard the sharp edge to Bea's reply.

A reply that implied she considered their lovemaking last night to be a part of that nightmare existence.

It had been Griffin's intention to apologise to her this morning at the earliest opportunity for the serious lapse in his behaviour and judgement but he now found himself bristling with irritation instead.

At the same time as he knew it was illogical of him to feel regret for his own actions, but feel offended when Bea expressed she felt the same way.

If only Christian were not here, perhaps he might have tried to explain to Bea *why* he regretted it.

'If you will both excuse me?' As if aware of Griffin's thoughts, Sutherland placed his napkin on the table before rising to his feet, an expression of studied politeness on his face as he bowed to them both. 'It is such a pleasant morning, I believe I will take a stroll about the grounds.'

'I believe I asked last night to be given answers this morning?' Bea reminded tightly.

'Not now, Bea.' Griffin glanced pointedly at Pelham as he stood beside the breakfast salvers.

'Then when?' she demanded, eyes glittering. 'Very well,' she bit out angrily when neither man answered her. 'As you are obviously no more inclined to answer my questions this morning than you were last night, I believe I will join His Grace for a walk in the grounds.' Bea also rose to her feet, her napkin falling to the floor in her haste. 'If I would not be intruding?' she added to Sutherland before bending to retrieve the napkin.

Griffin and Christian exchanged a glance over the top of Bea's bent head as Griffin rose politely to his feet. Christian's look was questioning, while his own was of scowling displeasure at the thought of Bea alone in the garden with the other man.

An emotion Griffin knew he did not have the right to feel. He was not truly Bea's guardian, so could not object. He would not, could not, claim to be Bea's lover, so again he had no right to object to her enjoying the company of another man.

'I will accompany you, Bea, if you wish to go outside,' he offered instead.

'No, thank you.' Bea did not as much as glance at him. 'Your Grace?' She looked at Sutherland.

'I have no objection if Griffin does not?' Christian still eyed him questioningly.

Bea bristled resentfully at the mere suggestion that it was any of Griffin's business what she chose to do after the conversation she had overheard between the two men last night. Griffin had dismissed not only her, but also their lovemaking, as a mistake that meant nothing to him.

'I believe I shall stroll in the garden, in any case,' she stated determinedly. 'If we should happen to meet, Your Grace—' she glanced coolly at Seaton '—then perhaps we might stroll along together.'

'Bea—'

'If you will excuse me, I believe I will go to my room and collect my bonnet.' Again Bea ignored Griffin as she turned on her heel and marched determinedly from the room, her head held high.

'As I remarked last night,' Sutherland mused softly as he watched her leave, Pelham following, at Griffin's discreet nod for the butler to do so, 'Bea is a fascinating young woman.'

'And as I replied, you are to stay away from her.' Griffin glared.

'Can I help it if she prefers my company to yours today?' the other man drawled dryly.

'This is not a laughing matter, Christian.'

'I could not agree more.' Sutherland sobered grimly. 'Will you accompany Bea on her walk, or shall I? In any case, she should not be left to stroll outside in the grounds alone and unprotected,' he added firmly.

Griffin eyed him sharply. 'The threat is still near, then?'

'Very near.'

He breathed his frustration with the situation. 'If you would only confide—'

'I cannot, Griff!' The refusal obviously caused Christian some discomfort. 'There are other lives at risk, and for the moment all I can do is offer to assist you in keeping Bea safe.'

Griffin could see by the strain about Sutherland's eyes and mouth that his regret was genuine over his enforced silence. 'Can you at least reassure me that Bea will be safe as long as one of us is with her?'

'I— Not completely,' the other man confessed. 'The stakes are high, Griff, and Bea may have information that is the key.'

'As I explained to Maystone in my note, she has no memory of who she is, or the events before her abduction.'

'But those memories could return at any moment,' Sutherland reasoned. 'And we believe there are people who would like to ensure they do not.'

Griffin shook his head. 'I have had the estate workers keep constant watch for strangers since the night I found her wandering in the woods and brought her here. They have assured me they have seen no one who doesn't belong here in the immediate area.'

The other man raised blond brows. 'Then perhaps the people in question are not strangers?'

Not strangers? Did that mean that the person, or people, who had abducted and harmed Bea might belong to the village of Stonehurst? That one of his own neighbours, possibly one of the ones whom he had visited just days ago, might be in cahoots with Jacob Harker, whom Griffin was still convinced had been Bea's jailer?

It did make more sense if that were the case, than that Jacob Harker had randomly chosen one of Griffin's own woodcutters' sheds on the estate in which to hide and then mistreat Bea.

But which of his neighbours could have been involved in such infamy? One of those social-climbing couples he had visited, and whose only interest had appeared to be to show off their marriageable daughters to him? Or the jovial Sir Walter? One of Griffin's own ten-ants? Someone who actually worked here in the house?

If it was the latter, then surely there would have been another attempt to silence Bea before now.

'I believe you must be the one to accompany Bea this morning, Christian,' he murmured softly as he heard her coming back down the stairs after collecting her bonnet. 'While you are gone I will ride over to visit a neighbour who has invited me to come and admire his new hunter. It is a terrible bore, but there is always the possibility I might learn something new while I am there.'

'Which neighbour would that be?' Sutherland enquired casually.

Too casually?

Griffin studied his friend's face as he answered him. 'Sir Walter Latham.'

'I do not believe I have ever met the gentleman.'

Had Griffin imagined it, or had something flickered in his friend's eyes at mention of Sir Walter?

He found it hard to believe that Latham would involve himself in intrigue and kidnapping; Sir Walter cared only for his wife, his horses and his hounds—and not necessarily in that order!

He shrugged. 'Latham does not care for London society and prefers to remain in the country. Although I believe his wife was in London for the Season.' He could not keep the distaste from his voice as he spoke of the woman who had been such a close friend to Felicity.

'You do not care for Lady Latham?'

Griffin's jaw tightened. 'She was a friend of my wife.'

'Ah.' Christian nodded knowingly. 'No doubt the dislike is mutual, then?'

'Without a doubt,' he confirmed with feeling.

The other man chuckled wryly. 'Marriage is a complicated business, is it not?'

'Women in general are complicated, I have recently been reminded.' Griffin grimaced.

The other man smiled. 'Have no fear, Griff, between the two of us we will ensure that no harm comes to your Bea.'

'She is not my Bea,' Griffin bit out harshly.

'No?'

'No,' he repeated emphatically.

No, nor would she ever be. Once Bea's memory was restored to her, and this business was over with, she would be able to return to whatever family she had left.

And the mysterious Michael.

'You really should not hold Griffin responsible for this present situation, you know,' the Duke of Sutherland remarked quietly, Bea's gloved hand resting lightly on his arm as the two of them strolled about the garden together.

No, Bea did not know.

She was grateful to Griffin for all he had done for her this past week, but that kindness could not excuse his deliberate silence over her identity. He did know now, she felt sure of it.

Nor could she forgive him for so easily dismissing the intimacies between them last night when he had spoken with Seaton.

Most of all she could not forgive him for that!

Their lovemaking had been beautiful. A true giving and receiving of pleasure such as Bea had never dreamt possible. A closeness she had believed must surely form a bond of some kind between the two participants.

Only for Griffin to have dismissed their time together so casually just minutes later.

Obviously it had not meant the same to him as it did to her.

Because he desired to make love to her but did not love her.

As Bea was so afraid she might have fallen in love with him.

And she was afraid, deeply so, that an unreciprocated love could only lead to heartbreak.

Her own heartbreak.

'I am sure Griffin is more than capable of putting forward his own defence if necessary, Your Grace,' she came back waspishly.

'But he will not.'

Bea glanced up at the handsome gentleman at her side. 'Why do you say that?'

He sighed. 'Because Griffin does not believe himself to be deserving of anyone's affection.'

Bea removed her hand from his arm as she turned fully to face him. 'I beg your pardon?'

Sutherland grimaced. 'Griffin and I have known each other for a long time, you understand. We were at school together.'

'I did not know that.'

He nodded. 'I do not believe I am being indiscreet by revealing that Griffin was placed in the school by his father when he was only eight years old. He was not a cruel man, merely elderly, and had been widowed since Griffin's birth. He did not, I believe, know quite what to do with his young son and heir, other than to place him in the competent hands of first a wet-nurse, then a nanny, and, finally, school.'

'But how lonely that must have been for Griffin!' Bea frowned at the thought of that lonely little boy, motherless, and sent away from the company of his father at such a tender age.

'Just so.' Seaton grimaced. 'We others did not join him until four years later. There were five of us altogether, all heir to the title of Duke. We were, and still are, a close-knit bunch. We became our own family, I believe, and have always looked out for each other,' he added enigmatically.

Bea's interest quickened. 'Then you also knew his wife?'

'I did, yes.' Seaton's expression became blandly unrevealing.

She nodded. 'Griffin loved her very much.' And no wonder, if he had led such a lonely childhood as Seaton had described. Griffin must have been so gratified to have someone of his own at last. Someone to love and want him.

Blond brows rose. 'Did he tell you that?'

'Well, no.' Bea frowned. 'But surely it is obvious?'

'How so?'

She shrugged. 'I understand it has been six years since his wife's death, and he has not re-married in that time.'

'Perhaps that is because one marriage was enough?' the Duke drawled.

Bea gazed at him speculatively. 'But surely it was a happy marriage?'

'I believe that is something you must ask Griffin, not me.'

'He refuses to talk to me of his marriage or his wife.'

'And I will not speak of it, either.' Sutherland grimaced. 'My only reason for discussing Griffin with you at all is in an effort to persuade you not to think too harshly of him for his silence about you. We have been, all five of the Dangerous Dukes, bound in our actions these past five years by a higher authority,' he added softly.

Other than God—and Bea did not believe Griffin or Christian Seaton to be overly religious men—what higher authority could there possibly be than a duke of the realm? Oh.

Bea looked sharply up at Seaton as she searched his handsome face for some indication that her surmise was correct. His expression, as he steadily returned her gaze, remained infuriatingly bland.

And yet the idea persisted that Griffin and his four closest friends had all—perhaps still?—worked in some way for the Crown.

It would explain so much about Griffin. The deft and efficient way in which he had dealt with her own unexpected and unorthodox appearance into his life. The fact that he had connections in London, like Lord Maystone, whom he might call upon discreetly to help him in discovering her identity.

It was perhaps also the reason Griffin had never married again; working secretly for the Crown could no doubt be a hazardous occupation, even in times of peace, as it now finally was. Already a widower, he was not a man who would allow his own actions to risk making his wife a widow.

Could that be the reason he was choosing to discourage her own affections?

No, it was more likely that Griffin simply did not feel that way about her.

But the rest of it?

Oh, yes, knowing Griffin she could well believe the rest of it.

Griffin was above all a man of honour, of deep loyalties, and once that loyalty had been given she had no doubt that he would never betray it. For anything or anyone.

'I see.' She nodded slowly.

'I hope that you do.' Sutherland gave a slight inclination of his head. 'Griffin is a good man, and I should not like to see you treat him with unnecessary harshness.'

Bea gave a rueful shake of her head. 'I believe you mistake our friendship, Your Grace. Circumstances have put Griffin in the role of an older brother to me, or—or an uncle.'

Blond brows rose up to the Duke's hairline. 'I trust you do not truly expect me to believe that?'

Bea could feel the blush in her cheeks at

thoughts of last night. 'Whatever Griffin has said to you in regard to me—'

'I am sure you know him better than to believe he would ever be so indiscreet as to discuss his friendship with a lady with a third party. Even one of his closest friends,' Seaton stated firmly. 'But I do have eyes, Bea, and the power of deduction, and I do not believe that Griffin was behaving as an older brother or an uncle to you when I arrived late last night.'

The heat deepened in her cheeks. 'That was all my own doing, not Griffin's.'

'Perhaps we should not discuss this any further, Bea?' Seaton suggested ruefully. 'Such conversations have the power of stirring the blood, I am far from London, and sadly the only beautiful woman in the vicinity is far more taken with my friend than she is with me.'

'You are a flirt, sir.' Bea could not help but laugh.

'Indubitably.' He gave an unrepentant grin as he once again placed her gloved hand upon his arm so that they might continue their walk about the gardens together.

But that did not mean that Bea did not continue to think of their conversation. For her heart to ache for the lonely little boy Griffin must once have been. For the sad and lonely widower he must also have been these past six years since he'd lost his wife.

For Bea to feel ashamed of her harshness towards him this morning, when she had spoken and treated him so coldly.

As no doubt the wily Duke of Sutherland had intended her to feel...

'Yes, Bea?' Griffin eyed her warily as she appeared in the doorway of the library, where he currently sat alone, drinking whisky and contemplating the unpleasantness of his visit to Latham Manor this morning.

She hesitated. 'I am not interrupting anything?'

'Only my thoughts,' he acknowledged dryly.

Lady Francesca had arrived back at Latham Manor the previous evening, and, as Griffin had quickly learnt, her acerbic tongue had not been in the least tempered by having spent the Season in London, followed by several weekend parties on her leisurely journey back into Lancashire.

'Thoughts I can well do without,' he added dismissively as he stood up and indicated that Bea should enter and take her usual seat by the fire, before he sat down opposite her.

He had missed her company this morning, truth be told, allowing him to realise that he had become accustomed to her presence in the library as he worked on estate papers. Seeing her strolling about the gardens before he left, her hand resting companionably on Christian's arm, had not improved his mood in the slightest. Finding Lady Francesca Latham back at home had only exacerbated his ill humour.

Nor had he learnt anything useful from the visit. Sir Walter was his usual jovial self, even more so now that his wife was returned to Lancashire, but the lady's jarring presence had not allowed for any private conversation between the two gentlemen.

The only good thing about the visit was that Griffin had not had to suffer through meeting Lady Francesca's whey-faced niece; she, no doubt having spent quite enough time in the company of her sharp-tongued aunt, had wisely chosen to remain a little longer at the home of one of her friends.

All in all, Griffin's day so far had not been a successful one. Bea had opted to eat lunch in her bedchamber, and Griffin had absented himself from afternoon tea on the excuse that he was busy working on estate business.

'I owe you an apology.'

Griffin tensed as he raised his gaze sharply to look searchingly at Bea. 'An apology for what?'

She sighed. 'I believe I was—unfair to you, both last night and this morning. The Duke of Sutherland was kind enough to explain a little about the restraints put upon the two of you, in regard to revealing my true identity.'

Griffin felt a certain satisfaction in hearing her still refer to Christian formally; he did not think he could have born to suffer through listening to Bea referring to the other man in a familiar way.

He was not so pleased with the rest of the content of her apology, however. 'And how did Christian do that?'

Bea sensed the reserve in Griffin's tone. 'His Grace was not in the least indiscreet, Griffin,' she hastened to reassure. 'He merely helped me to understand that there is more involved in all of this than my own personal wants and needs.'

'Indeed?'

Griffin sounded even more cool and remote when all she had wished to do was settle the unease that now existed between the two of them.

She had not forgotten overhearing his dismissal of their lovemaking last night, nor would she, but Christian Seaton *had* helped her to understand that there was a much broader picture to this situation, one that required she put her personal feelings of hurt to one side.

To be dealt with later.

She looked up at him quizzically. 'You would rather he had not said anything?'

Griffin would rather *he* had been the one to do the explaining.

Feelings of jealousy rearing their ugly head again?

Feelings he did not have the right to feel.

Feelings he would be unwise to feel.

He looked at Bea closely, noting the pallor to her cheeks. 'You have suffered no ill effects from our intimacy last night, I hope?'

'No, of course not.' Those cheeks immediately warmed with colour, her gaze avoiding meeting his. 'What ill effects should I have suffered?' she added waspishly.

Griffin, totally unfamiliar with a woman's pleasure, had no idea. It had merely been something for him to say once he had noticed her pallor. Something he obviously should not have said, when it seemed to have inspired a return of tension between the two of them.

He grimaced. 'I should not like to think that I had caused you any physical discomfort.'

'I have no idea what you are talking about, Griffin,' she dismissed impatiently, obviously in great discomfort at this moment, her arms tense as they rested on the brocade-covered arms of the chair, the knuckles of her fingers showing white as she tightly gripped the wooden ends.

He stood up restlessly. 'I am trying, in my obviously clumsy way, to put things right between us. To—to—I wish to have the old Bea returned to me!' he rasped.

Bea had to harden her heart to the frustration she could hear in his voice, knowing she could never again feel so at ease in his company after the events of last night. Not because she regretted them in the slightest, because she did not. It was overhearing Griffin voice *his* regrets over those events that now constrained her.

He loomed large and slightly intimidating over the chair in which she sat. 'Bea, if I could turn back the clock, and make it so that last night had never happened, then I would,' he assured her with feeling. 'I would do it, and gladly!'

Bea felt the sting of tears in her eyes. She had not thought that Griffin could hurt her more than he already had, but obviously she had been wrong.

A numbing calm settled over her. 'If anyone is responsible for the events of last night, then it is me. You did warn me against proceeding, but I refused to listen. You are not to blame, Griffin,' she repeated firmly as she stood up.

'I have made my apology, now if you will excuse me?'

'No!' Griffin reached out to grasp hold of her arms as she would have brushed past him. 'No, Bea, I will not, I cannot let you leave like this. Beatrix Stanton!' he bit out grimly as she kept her face turned away from looking at him directly. 'Your name is Lady Beatrix Stanton,' he repeated, no longer caring about Christian's warning of caution. Only Bea mattered to him at this moment, and putting an end to the estrangement between the two of them. 'You are the daughter of Lord James and Lady Mary Stanton, the Earl and Countess of Barnstable.'

Her face paled as she stared up at him for several long seconds with dark unfathomable eyes before finally crying out, 'Mamma! Pappa!' Before very quietly, and very gracefully, sinking into a faint in Griffin's waiting arms.

Chapter Eleven

'Did you not consider how dangerous it could be to tell an amnesiac the truth so bluntly?'

'Obviously I know now.' Griffin turned to scowl his impatience at Christian as the other man restlessly paced the length of the library and back.

Griffin sat beside Bea on the chaise, where he had placed her tenderly just minutes before, and now held one of her limp hands in his.

The other man frowned. 'I thought we had agreed last night that we would not tell Bea anything until after Maystone's arrival?'

'*You* agreed that with Maystone, not I,' Griffin growled. 'And in making that agreement the two of you seem to have forgotten that Bea is a person not an object, and that she at least had the right to know who she is.'

Christian ceased his pacing before slowly nodding. 'I apologise.' He grimaced. 'You are right, of course.'

Griffin raised surprised brows. 'I am?'

'Do not look so shocked, Griff, you are sometimes right, you know.' Christian smiled ruefully. 'I freely admit I was wrong to agree otherwise, no matter what Maystone's directive.'

'You have had a drastic change of mind since yesterday?' Griffin eyed him suspiciously.

Christian turned away. 'I discovered, while walking in the garden with Bea earlier today, that she is a lady about whom it is easy to feel…concern.'

Griffin scowled darkly at his friend's obvious admiration for Bea.

An admiration Griffin shared but now found himself resenting. Deeply. 'Is that the reason you chose to confide in her as to the nature of our association with Maystone?'

Sutherland looked uncomfortable. 'As I said, she is one in whom it is easy to…feel empathy.'

Griffin stiffened. 'Indeed?'

'Oh, not in that way, Griff,' Christian snapped his impatience. 'She is just so vulnerable, and so very alone. Damn it, Griff, you were the one making love to Bea when I arrived late last night, not I!' He scowled his exasperation with Griffin's scowl. 'And do you really know me so little that you believe me to be capable of ever attempting to usurp one of my closest friends in the play for a lady's affections?'

'I am not making a play for Bea's affections.'

'Perhaps that is because you do not need to do so!' the other man bit out tersely.

'You misunderstand the situation, Christian.' Griffin gave a shake of his head. 'Bea is grateful to me for my part in her rescue; that is all.'

Christian now eyed him pityingly. 'You are a fool if you believe that to be all it is.'

His eyes glittered in warning. 'I am not having this conversation, Christian.'

'Why on earth not? Griffin,' he continued in a reasoning tone, 'it is wrong of you to allow the events of the past to dictate how you behave now.'

'It is none of your affair, Christian.'

The other man continued to eye him in exasperation for several moments more before nodding abruptly and changing the subject. 'Do you think it possible that revealing Bea's name to her may have triggered a return of her memories?'

'Why?' Griffin looked at his friend through narrowed lids. 'What is it that she knows, Christian, that is of such importance Maystone sent you here almost immediately he received my letter? Why does he need to come here himself?'

Christian straightened. 'I have allowed that Maystone and I were wrong in deciding to keep Bea's identity from her until he arrives, but I will not concede any further than that. Please try to understand, Griff,' he added persuasively. 'I assure you Maystone is not being difficult, but he has his own reasons for remaining cautious. Reasons I cannot as yet confide.'

'I believe *I* might perhaps shed at least a little light on the matter,' Bea spoke softly as she opened her eyes and attempted to sit up on the chaise. A move hampered somewhat by the fact that one of her hands was being held firmly clasped in both of Griffin's. She avoided meeting his concerned gaze as she carefully but determinedly released her hand before sitting up and looking up at Christian Seaton.

'Lord Maystone mistakenly believes, as did my kidnappers, that I have information detrimental to their plans. Is that not so, Your Grace?'

Most, but not all, of Bea's memories had painfully returned to her the moment Griffin had revealed her full name. Along with the raw pain of losing the parents she had loved so dearly, both of whom had been killed during a winter storm when a tree had fallen onto and crushed their carriage with them both inside.

One memory she was profoundly grateful to have returned to her, however: neither Jacob Harker nor his accomplice had violated her. He had been an unpleasant man, and cruel in his care of her, but he had not physically harmed her in any way. Even the beatings had all been carried out by his accomplice, who had upbraided her jailer that day and so allowed Bea to overhear that his name was Jacob.

'Mistakenly?' Christian repeated slowly.

'Yes. Might I have a glass of water or—or perhaps some brandy, do you think?' Bea requested faintly as she lay her head back on the chaise, her mind once again swirling as some of the memories still danced elusively out of her reach.

'Of course.' Griffin stood up immediately to cross the room to where the decanter and glasses sat upon his desk top, pouring the dark amber liquid into a glass before returning.

Bea had managed to sit up completely in his absence, slippered feet placed firmly on the floor, her hands shaking slightly as she accepted the glass before taking a reviving sip of the drink.

So many of her memories had now returned to her. Her parents' death the previous winter was the most distressing.

They had been such a happy family. Her parents were still so much in love with each other, and it was a love that had included rather than excluded their only child. So much so that they had been loath to accept any of the offers of marriage Bea had received that previous Season, determined that their daughter should find and feel the same deep love for and from her husband. They wished for her to find a happy marriage, such as they had enjoyed together for twenty years.

After their sudden deaths her guardianship had been given over to her closest male relative— Oh, dear Lord!

'Bea?' Griffin prompted sharply.

She looked up at him with pained eyes. 'Please be patient with me, Griffin. It is such a muddle still inside my head.' Could it really be possible that the answer to her abduction and present dilemma was so close at hand?

Well, of course Bea's head was a muddle, Griffin accepted, feeling that he was in large part responsible for her present distress. Her face was deathly pale, her hands shaking slightly as she held tightly to the brandy glass. Christian had been quite right to upbraid him for his stupidity in having revealed Bea's name to her so unthinkingly that she had fainted from the shock.

At the time he had thought only of preventing her from leaving when things were so strained between the two of them. Instead his outburst had caused Bea immeasurable pain, and the distance between them now seemed even wider than it had been before he had spoken.

Much as it grieved him, Griffin realised that most of that distance was coming from Bea herself. Because her memories were too distressing? Or because she was still angry with him? Whatever the reason, Griffin had no choice but to respect her feelings, and so continued to keep his distance as Christian now took his place on the chaise beside Bea.

She gave the other man a tentative smile. 'I fear Lord Maystone's visit here may be a futile one in regard to myself,' she voiced regretfully. 'Even with my memories returning to me, I still do not have any idea what it is that my abductors thought I might know.'

'No idea at all?' Seaton looked disappointed.

'No,' she confirmed heavily before turning to Griffin. 'However, Griffin, I am now aware of who my—'

'Lord Maystone, Your Grace.' Pelham had appeared unnoticed in the library doorway, quickly followed by the visitor.

Bea turned in surprise to look at the visitor as he strode hurriedly into the room without waiting for Griffin's permission to do so.

Lord Maystone was a man possibly aged in his mid to late fifties, and he appeared a little travel-worn, as might be expected. But he was a handsome man despite his obviously worried air, with his silver hair and upright figure.

Bea did not recall ever having seen or met him before this evening.

Griffin scowled darkly as he looked across the room at Maystone. 'It's about time you arrived and gave an explanation for this whole intolerable situation!' He turned all of his considerable anger and frustration onto the older man.

'Griff—'

'I will thank you not to interfere, Christian.' Griffin eyed his friend coldly.

'I believe Aubrey might be in need of some refreshment before we do or say anything further?' Christian pointedly reminded Griffin of his manners.

Griffin shot his friend an irritated glance before turning to the silently waiting butler. 'Another decanter of brandy, if you please, Pelham, and possibly some tea,' he added with a glance at Bea, waiting only long enough for the butler to depart before speaking again. 'Neither I, nor Bea, I am sure, appreciate this ridiculous need you feel for secrecy, Maystone.'

'Griffin!' Bea was now the one to reprove him sharply as she stood up quickly to cross the room to Aubrey Maystone's side. 'Can you not see that Lord Maystone does not look at all well?'

She placed her hand gently on the older man's arm as she looked up at him in concern.

Griffin *had* noticed that Maystone looked slightly pale about the mouth and eyes, but he had assumed it was from the exhaustion of travelling so far and so quickly at his advanced years.

On closer inspection Griffin could also see that the older man had lost weight since he'd last seen him. To a considerable degree: his face was thinner, his jowls no longer firm, and his well-tailored clothing seemed to hang loosely upon his upright frame.

'Come and sit down, My Lord,' Bea encouraged gently, her arm gentle beneath May-stone's elbow as she guided him over to sit on the chaise.

'I am sure I shall feel perfectly well again soon, my dear.' Maystone patted Bea's hand reassuringly as she sat down beside him. 'Possibly after I have drunk a reviving glass or two of brandy.'

'Griffin?' Bea prompted pointedly, her attention and concern all on Aubrey Maystone.

Griffin caught the mocking glint in Christian's eyes as he moved to pour Maystone a brandy. As if the other man found Bea's somewhat imperious behaviour towards him amusing. Or, more likely, Griffin's reaction to it...

As far as he was concerned, this situation had already caused more than enough of an upset between himself and Bea, and he did not intend to tolerate much more of it. His scant patience had come to an end.

He moved stiffly away to stand before the window once he had handed over the glass of brandy to Maystone. 'I assure you, I am nowhere near as tolerant of this situation as Bea!'

'Griffin!'

'Griff!'

He scowled as he was simultaneously reprimanded by both Bea and Christian.

'Rotherham is perfectly within his rights to feel irritated by my request for secrecy.' Lord Maystone sighed deeply once he had swallowed a large amount of the brandy in his glass and some of the colour had returned to his cheeks. 'It is—' He broke off as Pelham returned with a tray carrying the second decanter of brandy, the pot of tea also in evidence. 'This is something of a lengthy tale, so I suggest we all make ourselves comfortable by sitting down and having tea or a brandy while I tell it,' he suggested heavily once the butler had departed at a nod from Griffin.

Bea continued to sit on the chaise beside the older man as Griffin first poured a cup of tea for her and placed it on the table near her, before replenishing Lord Maystone's glass, and then pouring brandy into two more glasses for himself and Christian, those two gentlemen then taking up occupancy of the chairs on either side of the fireplace.

There were several significant things she

had now remembered that she needed to discuss with Griffin, but perhaps those things would become clearer to her, to all of them, once Lord Maystone had told his lengthy tale.

She believed there was something else beneath Lord Maystone's obvious pallor and fatigue. Possibly an air of despair? Or perhaps even grief?

'Firstly, my Lady Bea,' Maystone began wearily, 'let me apologise to you for your having innocently become involved in this situation.'

She squeezed his arm reassuringly. 'I do not believe that it is your apology to make, My Lord, but that of the people responsible for my abduction and imprisonment.'

He grimaced. 'Nevertheless, I might have done something to prevent it. I am not sure what,' he added distractedly, 'but... Are you aware that I work within the Foreign Office?'

'I am, yes.' Bea gave Griffin a sideways glance from beneath her lashes.

Maystone nodded. 'Then I must also reveal that both Rotherham and Sutherland have for some time kindly assisted me in my less public work for the Crown.'

'I am aware of that also, Lord Maystone.' Bea turned away from Griffin's scowl to give the older man a reassuring smile. 'I am sure that you can appreciate it was necessary, for my own protection, that I be made aware of it?'

'I am sure Griffin acted only for the best.'

'I was the one to inform Lady Bea of the reason for my hurried presence here, not Griffin,' Seaton interjected decisively.

Lord Maystone's brows rose. 'Indeed?'

'Could we just get on with this?' Griffin glared his impatience over the delay; he just wanted to get this whole sorry business over and done with.

So that he might talk alone with Bea.

So that he might apologise for upsetting her earlier.

So that he might *be* alone with her.

He had always enjoyed Christian's company in the past, and the same was true of Aubrey Maystone, but here and now they both represented a deepening of that barrier between himself and Bea that he found so intolerable.

'Of course.' The older man sighed as he turned back to Bea. 'Several months ago there was a plot to assassinate the Prince Regent. A plot that was effectively foiled, my dear,' he added as Bea gasped and raised a hand to her throat. 'With the aid of Rotherham, Sutherland, and several other worthy gentlemen.' He nodded. 'After which, most of the perpetrators were found and arrested.'

'But not all?'

Griffin had long appreciated Bea's intelligence, and he could see it had not failed her now either, and that she was beginning, if not completely, to understand the restraints that had been placed upon his own conversations with her this past week.

'Not all, unfortunately,' Maystone acknowledged heavily. 'We have all of us been attempting, these past few months, to find those of the plotters who have infiltrated society itself. Do not be alarmed, my dear.' He placed a reassuring hand on Bea's arm as she drew her breath in sharply. 'I am sure you are perfectly safe here with both Rotherham and Sutherland to protect you.'

Griffin sincerely hoped that was the case, although he still suspected—and feared—that Jacob Harker was in hiding somewhere within the district.

It made no sense to him, with Bea now free and able to talk of her captivity, to assume that the other man would have completely disappeared from the area. Finding Bea, and possibly silencing her once and for all, would now be Harker's mission. After all, he could have no idea that Bea had suffered a temporary loss of her memories following the trauma of her abduction and frightening escape.

Nor did Griffin believe, with the information Christian had imparted to him, that Harker was acting upon his own initiative.

One, or perhaps more than one, other person was most assuredly in control of these events.

'My concern was not for myself,' Bea now assured Lord Maystone huskily; in truth, her present alarm was all on Griffin's behalf upon learning that he had been involved in the risky business of preventing a plot to assassinate the Prince Regent.

That Griffin might have been killed before she'd even had opportunity to meet him.

'What a sweet and caring child you are.' Lord Maystone smiled at her warmly before that smile turned regretful. 'Which only makes my guilt all the deeper regarding my own involvement in your sufferings— Not her abduction, Rotherham.' He frowned as Griffin tensed in his chair. 'Do give me a little credit, please. I was not even aware of Lady Bea's abduction until after you wrote and told me of it.'

'But you most certainly knew something was afoot,' Griffin put in testily. 'As is someone else; Bea's real guardian must also have been aware of it when she completely disappeared.'

'Griff—'

'Allow him to have his say, Sutherland.' Maystone sighed. 'Truth be told, I have handled this situation very badly, and as a consequence I deserve any approbation Griffin may care to lay at my feet.'

'I disagree.'

'Enough!' Griffin rose restlessly to his feet. 'Will you please just state the events, Maystone, and cease leaving Bea and I in this infernal state of uncertainty?'

Bea did not rebuke him this time; she knew from the pallor of his face and the nerve pulsing in his tightly clenched jaw that Griffin really was at the end of his patience.

And who could truly blame him? He had no doubt initially travelled to his country estate with the intention of enjoying some peace and quiet. Instead he had happened upon a woman in the woods who must have appeared to him to be deranged, quickly followed by the arrival of the Duke of Sutherland and now Lord Maystone. The poor man must have thought himself caught in the middle of bedlam this past week.

With no end to his suffering in sight.

He also had no idea as yet that Bea had now remembered the name of her guardian.

Lord Maystone emptied the rest of the brandy from his glass, his voice flat and unemotional when he spoke again. 'Three weeks ago an eight-year-old child was abducted, taken from his home, his parents and his family, for the sole intention of using the threat of taking his life as leverage in gaining access to certain information that might, indeed undoubtedly would, help in their cause against the Crown.'

'Good God!' Griffin breathed softly.

Maystone looked up at him with bloodshot eyes. 'That child is my grandson.'

Griffin closed his eyes in shame for his earlier rebukes and the anger he had shown towards Maystone since his arrival.

The man's grandchild had been abducted, his life threatened.

As Bea's had.

No wonder Maystone had added two and two together—his grandson's abduction followed by Griffin informing him Bea had suffered the same fate—and come to the conclusion of four!

Especially so when Griffin had stated in his letter to Maystone that there was a possibility that Jacob Harker, known to have been involved in the plot to assassinate the Prince Regent, and a man who just a few weeks ago had been seen in the area of Stonehurst, might have been involved in Bea's abduction and imprisonment. Bea's memory of the man's name being Jacob had, as far as Griffin was concerned, confirmed that suspicion, which he had also stated in his letter to Maystone. That had obviously caused both Sutherland and Maystone to travel so quickly to Stonehurst.

And no wonder, if Maystone's own grandson had also been abducted and kept prisoner.

Had the boy been kept a prisoner, or was there the possibility that he was already—?

The idea the boy might already be dead was so unthinkable that Griffin could not even finish the thought.

Although Maystone's bloodshot eyes and severe weight loss would seem to imply the older gentleman had also thought of that possibility these past agonising weeks. Far too often.

Griffin straightened briskly. 'The kidnappers have made their demands for the boy's release and safe return?'

'Most certainly,' Maystone confirmed leadenly. 'Demands with which I cannot possibly comply.'

'Oh, but—'

'I know what you are going to say, my dear.' Lord Maystone squeezed Bea's hand in understanding. 'But you must understand that my first loyalty has always been, must always be, to the Crown I have served all these years.'

No, Bea did not understand. A boy's life was at stake, this gentleman's own grandson— surely it was worth anything to have him returned safely to his family?

She gave a firm shake of her head. 'I admire your loyalty, of course, but there must be some way in which you can maintain that loyalty and still rescue your grandson?'

'We must respect Lord Maystone's views, Bea.' Griffin had easily seen and recognised that stubborn set to her mouth as the precursor to her frankly stating her own views on the subject.

'Why must we?' She stood up abruptly, those flashing blue eyes now including him in her anger. 'We are talking of a little boy, Griffin,' she added emotionally. 'A little boy who has been taken from his parents, from all that he loves. He must be so frightened. So very, very frightened.' Her hands were so tightly clasped together her knuckles showed white, as she so obviously lived through memories of her own abduction and imprisonment.

When she had suffered through that same fear of death, of dying.

'You must remain calm, Bea.' Griffin quickly crossed the room to clasp her clenched hands within his own.

'I do not see why.' Tears swam in those pained blue eyes as she looked up at him. 'Consider how you would feel, Griffin, if the child who had been taken were your own? How you would feel if your own son had been snatched from—?' She broke off as there came the sound of choking, both of them turning to look at Aubrey Maystone.

Just in time to see him fall back against the chaise, a hand clutching at his chest, his face as white as snow.

Chapter Twelve

'I did not mean— I had not thought to distress Lord Maystone so much that he— I am so very sorry!' Bea buried her face in her hands as the falling of her tears made it impossible for her to continue.

'It is not your fault, Bea,' Griffin consoled huskily as he reached out to cradle her in his arms.

The two men had managed, between them, to carry Lord Maystone up the stairs to one of the bedchambers, and Bea, Christian, and Griffin were now all seated about the library as they waited for the doctor to come back down the stairs after attending to his patient. Christian reclined in an armchair, Bea and Griffin once again sat together on the chaise.

'It is my fault,' Bea sobbed. 'I should not have said— I should have thought.'

'Nothing you said tonight was anything Maystone has not already said to himself many times during this past three weeks, Bea,' Seaton assured her comfortingly. 'The man has been beside himself with worry, and I have no doubts that this prolonged strain, and these added days of travelling, are the only reason for his collapse tonight.'

'Why did he not confide in me?' Griffin gave a pained frown. 'We could all have assisted in searching— No,' he guessed heavily. 'I am sure one of the kidnappers' demands was for Maystone's silence on the affair.'

Indeed, Griffin had thought of Bea's accusation prior to Maystone's collapse: How *would* he have felt if it had been his child who had been taken? Would he have turned England upside down in an effort to find his son? Or would he have done what Maystone had done, and suffered in silence himself rather than put the child's life in jeopardy?

If he had known Bea prior to *her* abduction,

would he have been able to stay silent when she was taken, in the hopes it might save her life?

The answer to that was he had already been doing exactly that for this past week.

As had the man Michael for whom she had cried out in her sleep? The man whom she must surely now remember?

Perhaps that was what she had been about to tell Griffin earlier, when Maystone had arrived and interrupted her.

Christian stood up restlessly. 'Maystone decided that, as you were leaving to follow up the rumour of Harker's sighting in Lancashire, and the other Dangerous Dukes were all busy with their new marriages, it must be me that he took into his confidence in this matter.' He looked grim. 'It has been difficult enough for me, knowing there is a child's life at stake, so goodness only knows how Maystone has coped with this prolonged strain.'

'And the boy's parents?' Bea lifted her head from Griffin's chest, her cheeks tear-stained. 'They must be beside themselves with worry.'

'His mother is prostrate and his father sits

at her bedside a great deal.' Sutherland nodded grimly.

'But what do the kidnappers' people want?' Griffin frowned. 'Something from Maystone, obviously, but what?'

Sutherland gave a grimace. 'Initially they had hoped he would use his influence to persuade the Prince Regent and the government into allowing Bonaparte to reside in England.'

Griffin narrowed his eyes. 'We are all aware that cannot be allowed to happen.'

'Of course not,' Christian acknowledged briskly. 'As we are also aware, there is still the hope amongst Bonaparte's followers that if he did reside in England they might one day be able to put him back on the French throne.'

'But that is ludicrous! Is it not?' Bea looked at the two men uncertainly as they exchanged a pointed glance.

'It certainly will be once Bonaparte is safely delivered and incarcerated on—' Sutherland broke off abruptly, giving an impatient shake of his head. 'At the moment there are legal moves afoot by Bonaparte's followers, to ensure that he remains in England. That is something the

Crown and government simply cannot allow to happen.'

'Understandably,' Bea acknowledged softly.

Christian grimaced. 'That legal process has been deliberately delayed, for obvious reasons, so that—Suffice it to say that, for the moment, for the matter of a few more days only, it is still possible for Bonapartists in England to foil the arrangements made for his incarceration. After which they are no doubt hoping to see him safely returned to France, at which time a civil war will once again break out, allowing Bonaparte to prevail through the ensuing chaos.'

'But surely the French people have already spoken, by accepting the return of their King?' Bea did not pretend to know a great deal about politics, few ladies of her age did, but even she did not believe that the usurper Napoleon could reign without the will of the majority of the people.

Sutherland gave a rueful shake of his head. 'A number of French generals have spoken, as has the British government and its allies, but they alone are responsible for the Corsican's complete defeat, and returning Louis to his throne. Napoleon's charisma has always been such that no one with any sense believes it will be possible to proclaim the man thoroughly subdued until after he is dead.'

Bea eyed him curiously. 'You sound as if you might have met him.'

'I have recently had that dubious honour.' Christian nodded ruefully. 'I expected to dislike him intensely, for the mayhem he has created here for so many years, as well as on the Continent, and for the lives lost because of it, many of them my own friends. Instead, I am sorry to say, I found him every bit as intelligent and charismatic as he is reputed to be.' His jaw tightened. 'Enough so that I perfectly understand Maystone's concerns should he give in to the demands of his grandson's kidnappers, and so allowing the Corsican's followers opportunity to free him.'

'And these demands are?' Griffin asked softly.

Christian's shoulders slumped. 'Can you not guess?'

He nodded. 'They wish to know the secret

details and destination of Bonaparte's exile, so that they might intercede either before or during his journey.'

'Details Maystone is obviously completely aware of.' Christian gave an acknowledging inclination of his head. 'And time, unfortunately, is running out.'

Bea was unsure as to whether he meant time was running out for the plans of Bonaparte's followers or for Lord Maystone's grandson. Either way, determined steps must be taken to find the little boy and return him to his parents and grandfather, before it was indeed too late.

Just the thought of an eight-year-old boy suffering the same cruel imprisonment that she had was beyond bearing.

'Griffin?' she appealed.

Griffin had never felt as impotent as he did with Bea looking up at him so trustingly. As if she believed he was capable of solving this situation when Maystone and Christian had been unable to in the past three weeks.

But he dearly *wanted* to deserve that look of complete trust, to be the hero that Bea believed him to be.

He turned to Christian. 'Have you and Maystone made any progress at all?'

Christian grimaced. 'We have arrested several more people involved in the original assassination plot, but all claim to know nothing of the kidnapping of Maystone's grandson. Consequently they did not have any information on where the boy is being held. Your information of Lady Bea's abduction, so similar to that of Maystone's grandson, is the first real indication we have had that mistakes are being made. Desperation is setting in, and when that happens…'

'The whole begins to unravel,' Griffin finished with satisfaction.

'But I have told you both that I do not know why I was taken! That I do not know anything.' Bea hesitated. 'That is not completely true. I now know *where* I was when I was abducted!' Her eyes lit up excitedly. 'I know who was at the house party that weekend. Surely once I have told you their names it can only be a matter of time— You have both said there is no time!' She groaned her frustration.

Griffin frowned in thought. 'You were abducted from a house party?'

'Yes. Sir Rupert Colville and his wife had invited my aunt and I— I am such a fool!' Bea pounded the palm of her hand against her forehead. 'Griffin, I tried to speak with you earlier. I know now who my guardian is—' She broke off to look up at Seaton. '*That* is the reason you have kept your own counsel since you arrived! Why you have been so protective of me.'

'Yes,' he confirmed grimly.

'Would someone care to enlighten me?' Griffin raised an impatient brow.

Bea turned back and unthinkingly clasped both his hands in hers.

'It is Sir Walter Latham, who is my late mother's cousin and now my guardian!'

Griffin gave a start, pulling sharply away from Bea before standing up. 'Sir Walter?' he repeated disbelievingly. Bea was the niece Sir Walter had spoken of so affectionately? The niece who had been in London with her aunt but whom Latham now claimed to be staying with friends? 'But he has no interest in politics or society.' Griffin frowned. 'He is a pleasant and jovial enough fellow, but otherwise— You already knew of this connection, Christian, and said nothing?' he accused, recalling how he had sensed his friend's air of reservation when they had spoken of Sir Walter earlier.

The other man gave a frustrated shake of his head. 'The fact that Lady Bea is his ward does not make Sir Walter guilty of any more than negligence at the moment, in having failed to report her as missing. And there are often other reasons than kidnapping for a young lady's sudden disappearance,' he added dryly.

Griffin turned back to Bea. 'You said your aunt accompanied you to this house party?'

'Yes,' she confirmed hesitantly.

That Lady Francesca Latham, always so cold and mocking, might be involved in intrigue and kidnapping, Griffin certainly *could* believe.

Especially so, when only this morning she had told him herself that her niece had decided to stay with friends rather than immediately accompany her aunt to her new home to Lancashire.

Unless…

Unless he was allowing his own dislike of Lady Francesca, and her past influential friendship with his wife, to colour his judgement?

The possible explanation for Lady Francesca's lie, as to her niece-by-marriage's whereabouts, might be that she was under the same warning of silence as Lord Maystone if she wished to have her niece safely returned to them.

Did Sir Walter know of Bea's abduction too, but was keeping up his jovial front in an effort to prevent that truth from becoming public, also in an effort to protect the life of his niece?

There were far too many questions yet unanswered for Griffin's liking!

And he was prevented from asking any more of them as the doctor came back into the room with his report on Aubrey Maystone's state of health.

Apparently the older man had suffered a slight seizure of the heart, but would recover fully, in time. For the moment, it was best that Lord Maystone rest as much as possible.

'I believe I will go and sit with Aubrey for a

while,' Christian quietly excused himself once the doctor had gone.

Leaving Griffin and Bea alone together.

Bea was instantly aware of a change in the atmosphere, a charged tension totally unlike the one that had existed when they had all spoken together of the unfortunate situation regarding the Corsican usurper, and how the deposed Emperor seemed to be the connection between the two kidnappings.

Did Griffin feel that tension too?

A glance from beneath her lashes revealed his expression to be one of wariness. As if he feared what she might say to him.

It was ridiculous of him to feel wary of her. Admittedly, she was still hurt at overhearing his rejection of their lovemaking. But she could never be truly angry with Griffin. She cared about him too much for that to ever be true. He could not be blamed for not having that same depth of feeling for her.

'What are—?'

'Are you—?'

They both began speaking at once, both stopping at the same time.

Bea looked across at Griffin shyly as he politely waited for her to speak first. 'What are we to do next, do you think?'

'Regarding the recovery of Maystone's grandson?'

'What else?' she prompted softly.

What else indeed, Griffin acknowledged, knowing it was ridiculous of him to think that Bea would have any interest in discussing the subject of their closeness last night when she now knew exactly who she was.

Who Michael was.

It irked that as yet she had still made no mention of the other man in her life.

Out of embarrassment and awkwardness, perhaps, because of their own closeness last night?

Bea need have no qualms in that regard where Griffin was concerned; what had happened between the two of them had been madness. A wonderful sensual madness, but it had been madness nonetheless.

A beautiful young woman such as Lady Beatrix Stanton could have no serious interest in a man such as him. A man so many years older than her, also a widower, and still suffering the emotional scars of his disastrous marriage.

He nodded abruptly. 'I believe we will have to wait until we are able to consult with May-stone on that situation.'

'Of course we must,' Bea allowed. 'What were you going to ask me just now?'

Griffin frowned for a second, and then his brow cleared. 'Ah. Yes. I wondered if you have a fondness for your aunt Francesca?' he enquired with deliberate lightness; after all, his own dislike of the woman was personal, and might not be shared by others, least of all her niece-by-marriage.

Bea gave a husky chuckle. 'She is a little overwhelming, I concede. But I do not know her terribly well—my mother and Sir Walter were not close,' she explained at Griffin's puzzled expression. 'As such I did not have opportunity to meet either Sir Walter or Lady Francesca often until after my parents—until after they had both died,' she added quietly.

'I really am so sorry for your loss, Bea.' Griffin took a step towards her and then stopped himself; there was absolutely no point in causing further awkwardness between the two of them by taking her in his arms—most especially when he could not guarantee the outcome.

He seemed to be fighting a constant battle within himself where she was concerned. The need to be close to her, to make love to her again, was set beside the knowledge that he did not have that right. That Bea belonged to another man.

Even if she had chosen not to speak to him of that man, as yet.

How could she, when he had taken such liberties? When just to think of the two of them together last night must now cause her immeasurable embarrassment and guilt?

No, better by far that he respect her silence, and the distance now between them, rather than cause them both further embarrassment.

'Griffin, do you think that I should go to—?'

'No!' he protested violently.

Her eyes opened wide at his vehemence. 'You do not know what I was about to say.'

'Oh, but I do,' he assured her dryly. 'You

have shown yourself to be both a courageous and resourceful woman this past week.'

'I do not believe that to be true.' She shook her head sadly.

'Oh, but it is,' Griffin countered. 'You are very determined. What's more you have refused to allow fear to dictate your movements. Consequently it is not in the least difficult for me to reason that you are thinking of offering yourself up as human bait, by going to your uncle and aunt's home in the hope that one or both of them might give themselves away as being involved in this plot of treason and kidnapping.'

As that had been exactly Bea's intention, she could not help but feel slightly put out that Griffin had so easily guessed what she had been about to suggest. 'But surely it is the obvious answer to this dilemma? A way of knowing, without doubt, if one or both of my relatives are involved, when I am able to see their reaction to my safe and unexpected return?'

'And what if that should turn out to be the case? What of the danger to yourself?'

'What of the danger to that little eight-year-old boy?' she said, tears glistening in her eyes. 'Griffin, you do not believe that he might already be—'

'No,' Griffin assured her abruptly. 'Certainly not.'

Bea eyed him quizzically for several long seconds. 'You are not a very good liar, Griffin,' she finally murmured sadly. 'At least, not when you are speaking to me.'

He drew in a ragged breath as he thought of the abused state in which he had found Bea. For a young child to suffer such ill treatment would surely cause irrevocable emotional damage, as much as physical. Although they had no reason to suppose that Maystone's grandson would be beaten, the boy was being held to ransom, and not because he personally was in possession of knowledge wanted by his kidnappers, as Bea apparently had.

'You really have no idea of what it is you might have overheard to cause your abduction?'

'None at all.' She gave a pained grimace. 'As far as I recall, it was just a weekend party, with the usual bored group of people attending.'

Griffin wished he dare ask if Michael had been one of those people, but again knew it would not be fair to place Bea in such a place of awkwardness. 'We will find Maystone's grandson, Bea, have no fear,' Griffin stated with determination. 'And if anyone is going to visit the Lathams then it will be me,' he added grimly.

'But would it not look suspicious if you were to visit them again so soon?'

He smiled tightly. 'Not if my purpose was to make Sir Walter an offer for his new hunter. He will refuse, of course, and have the satisfaction of owning a piece of horseflesh he believes coveted by his neighbour.'

'You must be terribly good at the secret work you do for the Crown,' Bea murmured ruefully. 'That is what you and the Duke of Sutherland do for Lord Maystone, is it not?'

'We should not speak aloud of such things, Bea.'

'But why do you do it, Griffin?' She looked up at him in confusion. 'Why have you chosen to deliberately put yourself in danger?'

It had begun as a way for him to evade

thoughts of his failed marriage and his dead wife, but had all too soon become a way of life. One that he did not think of so very much any more, but merely accepted the assignments he was given. Such as he had in his search for Jacob Harker.

And instead he had found Bea.

She had, he realised, become a part of his household this past week. Someone that he looked forward to seeing across the breakfast table every morning. To spending the mornings in companionable silence with. To talking and arguing with over dinner, as they conversed on a number of subjects, some of which they did not agree on, and a larger number of which they did.

He could not imagine being here without Bea.

And yet he knew that she must leave him.

Not to go to the Lathams' as yet. Not until they had first ascertained if the Lathams were directly involved in Bea's kidnapping, and that of Maystone's grandson. Or if they were merely remaining silent regarding Bea's disappearance out of concern for their niece's safety.

But once that situation was concluded? Yes, then a home must be found for Bea, either by returning her to her uncle and aunt, or with some other relative if one or both of them should be revealed as being involved in these kidnappings.

'There is no one to care what I do, and so I do what has to be done,' Griffin answered her bluntly.

Bea *cared*!

She cared very much what happened to Griffin.

Now and in the future.

Even if he did not want or need her concern.

'That is unfortunate—Your Grace!' She turned concernedly to the Duke of Sutherland as he appeared in the doorway. 'How is Lord Maystone feeling now?'

He stepped into the room. 'He wishes to speak with both of you now, if that is convenient?'

'Why?' Griffin eyed the other man suspiciously.

Sutherland looked grim. 'Best you speak to Maystone, Griff.'

Griffin had a fair idea of what Aubrey May-stone wished to discuss with him—at this point in time the older man was feeling desperate enough to go to any lengths to achieve the return of his grandson.

Even suggesting, as Bea had already done, that her immediate return to the Lathams' home might bring forth the breakthrough in this impasse that was so sorely needed.

Chapter Thirteen

'Absolutely not! I will not hear of it!' Griffin barked furiously in reply to Maystone's suggestion. The older man was looking very pale and tired as he lay back against the pillows in one of the guest bedchambers at Stonehurst Park.

'But, Griffin—'

'I tell you I will not hear of it, Bea!' He turned that glare on her. 'Whatever it is that Bea is supposed to know, she has no knowledge of it now—' he turned back to the other two men '—and to even think of sending her back amongst that possible nest of vipers, completely unprotected, is totally unacceptable.'

'But she will not be unprotected,' Christian put in softly. 'It has been proposed that I will accompany Lady Bea, along with her maid.'

'She has no maid.'

'Then we shall find her one,' Christian said reasonably.

Bea could not bear to be the cause of contention between Griffin and the gentlemen, who were obviously two of his closest friends. 'It is no more than I offered to do myself just minutes ago, Griffin,' she reminded softly.

'And if you recall I turned down that offer. Unequivocally!' he came back fiercely.

'But surely you can see it is the only course of action that makes any sense?' she reasoned. 'I will go to Latham Manor, having travelled from my friend's house under the kind protection of the Duke of Sutherland. At which time, my aunt and uncle will then either react with gladness at my safe return after my abduction, and so proving their innocence. Or they will both sincerely thank the Duke of Sutherland for having safely returned me from my visit with friends, and we will know that in all probability my aunt has lied. It all makes perfect sense to me.'

'It makes *no* sense to me!' Griffin bit out as he ran an exasperated hand through his hair.

'But—'

'It is far too dangerous, Bea,' he ground out harshly as he continued to glare down at her. 'Added to which, I absolutely forbid it!'

She sat back in surprise, not only at the fierceness of Griffin's emotions, but also because he felt he had the right to forbid her to do anything.

Admittedly he had been claiming to be her godfather and guardian this past week, as a means of explaining her presence here at Stonehurst Park, but it was a sham at best, and a complete untruth at worst. Griffin could not seriously believe that tenuous arrangement gave him the right to forbid any of her actions?

'Have a care, Griff,' Christian warned ruefully as he obviously saw the light of rebellion in her eyes. 'It has been my experience, in my many dealings with my younger sister, Julianna, that it is a mistake for any man to forbid a strong-minded woman to do anything—unless he expects her to do the opposite. For myself, in regard to Julianna, I am more than gratified to have passed that particular responsibility over to Worthing!' He grinned ruefully.

Griffin drew in a harsh, controlling breath, well aware of the contrariness of a woman's actions; he had been a married man for a year, after all.

'This is all my fault,' Maystone rallied apologetically. 'For having suggested such a plan in the first place.' His expression gentled as he looked up at Bea. 'Perhaps Griffin is in the right of it, my dear, and we should not proceed with this.'

'Griffin is most certainly *not* in the right of it!' Bea stood up, her expression one of indignation, eyes glittering rebelliously as she glared at Griffin. 'Lord Maystone's suggestion is a sound one. And I shall do just as I please,' she added challengingly as Griffin would have spoken. 'I have no doubt I shall be perfectly safe under the protection of the Duke of Sutherland.'

That was one of Griffin's main objections to the plan!

Besides the obvious one of Bea deliberately placing herself in the path of danger.

Whether either of the Lathams were involved in her abduction or not, Bea's reappearance at their home would still leave her vulnerable to the people who had been responsible. To Jacob Harker, at the very least.

Besides which, if anyone was to act as Bea's protector then it should be him. In this particular situation that was an impossibility, when the Lathams lived but a mile away from Stonehurst Park, and he was supposed to be unacquainted with the Lathams' niece. And if Griffin could not be at her side, once she was returned to the uncertainty as to the innocence of the inhabitants of Latham Manor, then he could not, in all conscience, approve of Bea going there either.

Or bear the thought of her spending so much time alone with Christian.

Griffin knew his own nature well enough to realise he could be taciturn and brusque, and that his looks were not, and never would be, as appealing as Christian's. Just as he knew Bea could not help but be charmed by the man, as so many other women in society had been and still were, if the two of them were to be so much together at Latham Manor.

If Christian, charming and gentlemanly,

were perforce to become Bea's rescuer in Griffin's stead.

What made the situation worse was that Griffin knew how ridiculous it was for him to feel this way.

Even petty and childish.

Griffin knew he would be lying if he claimed to not already feel jealous at having to share Bea, first with Christian, and now with Maystone too.

This current conversation was a prime example of just how frustrating he found having this situation taken out of his control! 'I believe I should like to go to the library and discuss this alone with Bea, if you two gentlemen have no objection?' He eyed the other two men stonily.

'And if *I* should object?' In point of fact, Bea did not have any objections to going anywhere with Griffin, but she did resent his highhanded attitude in not so much as consulting with her on the subject.

He turned that stony gaze on her. 'Do you?'

She drew her breath in slowly, sensing, despite his chilling and controlled appearance, that Griffin was teetering on the edge of another explosion of temper. 'I merely wish you to have the courtesy of consulting me,' she finally replied softly.

'Very well.' His jaw had tightened. 'If you would care to accompany me to the library, Bea, so that we might discuss this matter further and in private?'

It was impossible, facing the three gentlemen as she was, for Bea to miss the knowing look that passed between Seaton and Lord Maystone, even if she did not quite understand it.

'By all means I will accompany you to the library, Griffin. Gentlemen.' She nodded politely to Sutherland and Maystone. 'But be aware, Griffin,' she added as he moved to politely open the door for her so that she might precede him out of the bedchamber, 'I have no intention of allowing myself to be bullied. By you or anyone else,' she warned as she swept past him and out into the hallway.

Was it even sane of him, Griffin wondered as he had to hold back a smile as he accompanied Bea down the curved stairs to the library, to feel both admiration and frustration for her at one and the same time?

Admiration for the way in which she had conducted herself just now.

And frustration with the light of determination he had seen so clearly in her eyes as she gave him that set-down.

'I am aware our conversation was interrupted earlier, Bea,' he remarked as he closed the library door firmly behind them. 'But nevertheless, I cannot have left you in any doubt as to my disapproval of this scheme.'

Bea faced him as she stood in the middle of the room. 'Even if it were to save the life of a small child?'

Griffin's hands were clenched together behind his back. 'I do not believe it sensible to save one life by putting the life of another at risk, no.'

She eyed him reprovingly. 'I am sure, during your own work for the Crown all these years, that you must have done so many times in the past?'

'I...' Griffin hesitated in order to draw in a deeply controlling breath.

He knew Bea too well now, realised that the remark he had intended to make—that he was a man, and so the situation was different—would only result in Bea becoming even more intransigent.

'I may well have done,' he conceded. 'But the risk to you in this situation is too great. Bea, you might conceivably have died of the cruel injuries deliberately inflicted upon you the last time you were held prisoner,' he added gruffly.

And instantly regretted it, as he saw the colour immediately leave her cheeks.

He stepped forward quickly to grasp her shoulders as she would have swayed. 'I did not mean to upset you by reminding you of such things,' he bit out. 'Can you not understand, Bea—' he attempted to temper his tone '—that I am concerned for your safety?'

Tears swam in her eyes. 'It would indeed be a pity to undo all the good work you have done this past week by tending my cuts and bruises and feeding and clothing me.'

Griffin drew back as if Bea had struck him.

Indeed, it felt as if she had just done so. 'That was an unforgivable thing for you to say, Bea.'

It was, Bea knew that it was. It was just that she'd felt so disconnected from Griffin since Christian Seaton's and Lord Maystone's arrival. As if the closeness the two of them had shared this past week had been completely rent asunder by the arrival of his other visitors.

She *missed* Griffin.

As she missed their previous closeness. Their conversations. Their bantering and occasional laughter. Their lovemaking.

But that was still no reason for her to have been so mean to Griffin just now.

She bowed her head in shame. 'I apologise, Griffin.' She looked up at him, tears blurring her vision. 'This is just such an awful situation for everyone, and I cannot bear the thought of that little boy being all alone, and suffering as I did. I want to *do* something to help him, Griffin.'

Griffin was well aware that she felt as impotent as he did over this situation. But, still, he could not bear the thought of her once again being placed in danger, and this time by a decision consciously made.

He knew he looked defeat in the face because of the depth of her determination. 'I do not suppose I can stop you if you have made your mind up to help.'

'Oh, thank you, Griffin!' She beamed up at him as she reached out to clasp both of his hands in her own. 'I will feel so much better about doing this if I have your blessing.'

Griffin was not sure she did have his blessing, but he did welcome the breaking of the tension that had existed between the two of them for most of today. As he welcomed her voluntarily touching him again.

He looked down at her gravely as his fingers tightened about hers. 'You will be careful, Bea? And you will accept Seaton's instructions in regard to your safety?' He almost choked over the directive, still far from happy that Christian would be the one to accompany Bea to Latham Manor, but knowing that he now had no choice, in the face of Bea's stubbornness, but to accept it with good grace.

Most especially so when he now held Bea's

hands in his own and knew himself bathed in the warmth of her smile.

'I will do as you ask.' Bea moved instinctively up on her tiptoes to kiss him lightly on the cheek, her own cheeks immediately becoming flushed and warm as she looked up at him shyly. 'I cannot thank you enough for being so very kind to me this past week, Griffin.'

A nerve pulsed in his tightly clenched jaw. 'You are a woman whom it is easy to be kind to.'

The two of them remained looking at each other for several long moments, before Bea broke the connection as she sternly reminded herself of the conversation she had overheard last night between Griffin and his friend. She must not make the mistake again of thinking that his kindness towards her, his concern for her welfare, was anything deeper than that of a man who cared deeply for others—hence his work for the Crown these past years—even if he did not care to show it in the often stern exterior he presented to the world at large.

She released his hands before stepping away. 'I shall need to go up to my bedchamber and pack what few belongings I now have. I shall have to give the excuse to my aunt and uncle that, having accepted the Duke of Sutherland's protection for the journey, the rest of my luggage will be arriving later by carriage,' she added with a frown.

Griffin still believed this whole concept, of Bea going to Latham Manor, was fraught with the possibility of mistakes being made, of someone getting hurt. Possibly Bea herself. Mistakes she, or Griffin, or even Christian, would not have any control over.

Which was not to say Griffin did not intend to find some way in which he might watch over her himself.

'Do not scowl so, Griffin!' Bea advised teasingly the following morning as she sat in the coach opposite Christian Seaton, prior to their departure for Latham Manor. She wore a pretty yellow bonnet over her curls to match her gown, with her hands and arms covered to the elbows by cream lace gloves.

She looked, in fact, to Griffin's eyes at least, a picture of glowing health and happiness. All of the visible bruising had now faded from her creamy skin, and her eyes shone brightly with the excitement of what she was about to do.

As she stepped willingly—even eagerly—into a possible lion's den.

Albeit with Christian at her side.

Griffin's jaw tightened as he looked at his friend, seated across the carriage from Bea. 'It is understood that at the first sign of danger you are to bring Bea away from there?'

The other man gave a mocking inclination of his head. 'Do not fear, Griffin,' he drawled as he stretched his legs out across the carriage. 'You may rest assured I shall take good care of our little Bea.'

Griffin's eyes narrowed at his friend's obvious mockery. 'You will send word immediately with Miss Baines if I am needed.' He nodded in the direction of the young woman sitting beside Bea. She was a niece to his housekeeper, Mrs Harcourt, who had agreed to accompany Bea to Latham Manor as her maid. 'I shall be visiting Sir Walter this morning, in any case.' He was also well aware that he might possibly arrive too late, if there was an immediate reaction to Bea's arrival. But this proposed visit to take another look at Sir Walter's hunter was the best that Griffin could come up with in the circumstances.

At least this way he might have opportunity to be formally introduced to Bea as Sir Walter's niece.

The irony of his eagerness now to be introduced to Sir Walter's niece, when he had not cared to meet the daughters and nieces of any of his other neighbours, was not lost on Griffin.

Nor was the possibility of Lady Francesca Latham being involved in the plot to secure Bonaparte's freedom.

Again Griffin questioned as to whether or not he was being influenced in this suspicion by his personal dislike of the woman. Lady Francesca had been far too much of a negative influence on his late wife, he suspected, in regard to their marriage, and him. And she'd enjoyed being so, if the mocking smiles Lady Francesca had so often given Griffin were an indication.

'Is that altogether wise, Griffin?' Christian

frowned at Griffin's proposed visit to Latham Manor.

Wise, or otherwise, it was Griffin's intention to visit shortly after Christian and Bea had arrived. 'I shall be calling upon Sir Walter this morning.' He nodded.

'As you wish.'

'It is exactly as I wish.' Griffin gave another terse nod before stepping back and closing the carriage door.

His last sight of Bea as she left Stonehurst Park—and him—was as she turned her head away from the window in order to answer something said to her by Christian.

'Stay calm, Griffin,' Aubrey Maystone advised softly half an hour later as he and Griffin travelled down the driveway of Latham Manor in the ducal coach.

Griffin stilled immediately as he became aware of the fact that he was sitting on the edge of his seat, as well as tapping his hat impatiently against his thigh. An impatience exacerbated by the fact that he had been forced to travel by coach at all, out of concern for Maystone's health, when he would have much preferred the faster travel of horseback.

Truth was, he would have preferred to call upon the Lathams by himself, and he had told Maystone as much when the older gentleman had announced his intention of rising from his bed and accompanying him.

Maystone was not to be gainsaid, however, and in the end Griffin had no choice but to capitulate when he could see how pale and agitated the older man was in his need for news of his young grandson.

As agitated, in fact, as Griffin was in regard to news of Bea's reception on her arrival at Latham Manor.

He shot Maystone an impatient glance. 'I warn you now, I cannot answer for my actions if anyone has harmed so much as one hair upon Bea's head!' His teeth were clenched, a nerve pulsing in the tightness of his jaw.

The older man's expression softened. 'Perfectly understandable, when you are in love with her.'

'I— What?' Griffin looked at the other man incredulously. 'Of course I am not in love with

Bea,' he denied harshly. 'I am concerned for her safety, that is all.'

'Of course you are.'

'I have had to suffer enough of Christian's sarcasm these past two days, and can quite well do without your adding to it!' Griffin scowled darkly.

The older man gave an acknowledging nod. 'It was not intended as sarcasm. Very well, I will say no more on the matter,' he acquiesced as Griffin continued to glare coldly across the carriage at him, before politely turning away to look out of the window at the trees lining the driveway.

Leaving Griffin alone with his thoughts.

Was he in love with Bea?

Of course he was not! The mere idea of it was preposterous, ridiculous.

Preposterous and ridiculous or not, was it possible that the feelings of jealousy, of possessiveness, which Griffin so often felt where Bea was concerned, might indeed be attributed to a growing affection for her?

No!

He did not love Bea or any other woman. Nor would he ever do so.

And Bea?

Griffin had no choice, once this present situation had resolved itself, other than to allow Bea to return to Michael. The man she obviously loved.

After which she would likely not give Griffin so much as a single thought. Unless it was out of gratitude for having saved her from her abductors. And for having returned her safely to the man she would no doubt give the rest of her life, and her love, to.

'We are arrived, Griffin,' Maystone announced softly as the carriage came to a jostling halt at the end of the driveway.

Griffin barely managed to contain his impatience long enough to allow his groom to open the carriage door, and then wait while Maystone preceded him down onto the cobbled driveway, before quickly jumping down from the carriage himself.

He drew in a deep and steadying breath as he placed his hat back upon his head to look up at the grim grey-stone visage of Latham Manor.

Knowing that Bea was somewhere inside this inhospitable-looking house…

Chapter Fourteen

'The Duke of Rotherham and Lord Aubrey Maystone,' the Lathams' butler announced from the doorway of the salon in which Bea, Christian and Sir Walter Latham sat together drinking the tea she had recently poured for them.

She and Seaton had arrived at Latham Manor just thirty minutes previously, to be greeted enthusiastically by Sir Walter. And in such a manner as to indicate that the gentleman had no knowledge of Bea's abduction, but had in fact believed her to be visiting with friends.

Thus confirming Lady Francesca's guilt?

Unfortunately they had no answer yet as to whether that was indeed the case; Lady Francesca was out this morning, paying courtesy calls upon her neighbours.

The question now was whether or not Lady Francesca had actively lied to her husband regarding the reason for Bea's disappearance two weeks ago. Or whether that lady herself believed that Bea had eloped, and she had merely told the lie of Bea visiting with friends in order to prevent her husband from worrying about his ward.

Sir Walter's pleasure in having Bea back with him could not be doubted, nor his gratitude to the Duke of Sutherland for having escorted her here.

Now that Bea's memory was returning to her she had recognised the rotund gentleman on sight, of course. And remembered him with affection, if not great acquaintance; her real acquaintance with Sir Walter had only occurred upon her parents' deaths last winter, when he and Lady Francesca had attended the funeral and then, as her guardians, taken her to live with them in their London home. Sir Walter had not remained long in Town with the two ladies once the Christmas holiday was over, preferring to return to his country estate and his pursuits there.

Bea stood up now as Griffin entered the salon first, followed more slowly by a white-faced Lord Maystone; surely that gentleman should not have come here at all, when he had been ordered by the doctor to rest. Although Bea had no doubt Lord Maystone would feel less anxious if he was allowed to actively do something in regard to bringing about the return of his missing grandson.

'Your Grace!' Sir Walter greeted warmly, obviously slightly overwhelmed by the visit of yet more exulted company this morning.

'Latham.' Griffin nodded abruptly. 'My recently arrived guest, Lord Aubrey Maystone,' he introduced just as tersely, having eyes for no one else but Bea as she stood so still and composed across the room.

He could read nothing from her expression. Nor, as he glanced at Christian, did his friend give him any more than a shrug. One that seemed to imply frustration, rather than an indication that Christian had come any closer to learning the truth of this situation.

And the reason for that frustration soon became obvious as Sir Walter apologised because his wife, Lady Francesca, was presently not at home.

Lady Francesca's many absences from home might be perfectly innocent, but Griffin sensed, more than ever, that the woman had information that would give them the answers to the reason for Bea's abduction.

And might also lead to the whereabouts of Maystone's young grandson.

'More cups, if you please, Shaw,' Sir Walter instructed the butler once he had made Aubrey Maystone's acquaintance. 'I am sure you gentlemen must both already be acquainted with my guest, the Duke of Sutherland,' he continued jovially. 'And please allow me to introduce my ward, Lady Beatrix Stanton.'

Griffin nodded abruptly to Christian before he quickly crossed the room to where Bea now stood. As if he had been drawn there by a magnet.

As indeed he had been; just this short time of Bea being out of his sight, out of his protection, had been a sore trial to his already frayed temper.

'A pleasure to meet you at last, Lady Beatrix.' He took the gloved hand she held out to him, holding her gaze with his as he brushed his lips across her knuckles while maintaining that hold upon her hand. 'Sir Walter omitted to mention your beauty when he spoke of you.'

To say that Bea felt reassured upon seeing Griffin again, even though it had only been half an hour or so since the two of them had parted, would be putting it too mildly. His mere presence had the effect of making her feel safe.

Even if that feeling of safety was a false one.

Inside Latham Manor was, to all intents and purposes, almost as comfortably appointed as Stonehurst Park. Not quite so grandiose perhaps, but the furnishings were lavish, the paintings and statuary were also beautiful.

Even so there was a chill to the atmosphere in this house that had not been present in Griffin's home, despite his not having visited there for some time.

That chill seemed to emanate from the fabric of the house itself, as if placed there by its owners.

'I agree, dear Beatrix is everything that is charming and lovely, Your Grace,' Sir Walter acknowledged Griffin's compliment warmly.

Sir Walter appeared to be everything that was jovial and friendly, leading Bea to conclude that the chill of the house must have come from Lady Francesca.

During their months spent in London together Bea could not say that she had found the other woman to be of a type she might make into a bosom friend, but she had not found her to be unfriendly either. They were merely of a different age group, Lady Francesca nearing forty years of age, and Bea not yet twenty. Nor did Lady Francesca appear to possess the maternal instinct that might have drawn the two women closer together. That the Lathams' marriage was childless perhaps accounted for the latter.

Bea had no idea if she was merely being fanciful about her aunt-by-marriage, or allowing some of Griffin's obvious aversion to Lady

Francesca to influence her own feelings towards the wife of her guardian.

No doubt they would all learn more upon that lady's return.

Bea felt a blush warm her cheeks as she became aware that the other three gentlemen in the room were now eyeing her and Griffin curiously. No doubt that was because Griffin still had a hold of her hand.

'May I pour you two gentlemen some tea?' She deftly slid her fingers from between Griffin's, before once again making herself comfortable on the sofa, waiting until Shaw had entered the room and placed the extra cups on the tea tray in front of her before pouring more of the brew.

She was barely aware of Lord Maystone's acceptance as Griffin chose that moment to make himself comfortable on the sofa beside her.

The hard length of his thigh pressed warmly against her own.

'Tea would be perfect, thank you, Lady Beatrix,' he accepted huskily.

Bea turned slightly to give him a sideways

frown from beneath her lashes. The two of them were supposed to have only now been introduced to each other, and from what she had gathered of Griffin's relationship with his neighbours, and his indifference towards re-marrying, she did not believe he usually singled out any of his neighbours' nieces—for his particular attentions. Much more of this and Sir Walter would be demanding that the Banns be read on the morrow!

Aware of the reason for Bea's censure, Griffin moved his thigh slightly away from her own. But he could not bring himself to move away from her completely, finding some comfort in at least being close to her.

'I hear you have recently added a fine grey hunter to your stable, Sir Walter?' Aubrey Maystone smoothly stepped into Griffin's breech in manners after receiving his cup of tea. 'You must allow us to see this fine horse-flesh before we depart!'

Griffin took advantage of Sir Walter's fulsome praise of the other man's hunter in which to talk quietly with Bea. 'You are well?'

'Quite well, Your Grace,' she replied quietly

as she handed him his tea. 'We only parted a short time ago,' she added even more softly.

Griffin put the cup and saucer down on the table beside him untouched as he kept the intensity of his gaze fixed upon Bea. 'And I have hated every moment of it!'

Bea gave him a searching glance, cautioning herself not to read too much into Griffin's statement; he could just be once again referring to the danger she had placed herself in rather than any deeper meaning.

Such as that he loved her as she surely loved him?

Bea had known it for a fact the moment the carriage had pulled away from Stonehurst Park earlier this morning. Had felt an ache in her heart such as she had never known before. An emptiness that could only be filled by Griffin's presence.

She loved him.

Not because she was grateful to him for having rescued her. Not because he had continued to protect her once he'd realised she had no idea who she was. Nor because they had made such beautiful love together.

She loved Griffin.

All of him. The bad as well as the good.

His manners, for instance, could be exceedingly rude. His nature could occasionally be morose, even terse. As for his suspicions concerning her friendliness towards the gardener, Arthur Sutton, and Christian Seaton—they had been altogether unacceptable.

But there was a kindness to Griffin, a caring, that he hid beneath that gruff exterior. Perhaps because of his lonely childhood. Or the sad end to his marriage. Whatever the reason, Bea saw beneath that gruffness to the man beneath, and she loved him.

Unreservedly.

When all of this was over she did so hope that the two of them could remain friends, at least. She did not think she could bear it if they were to never see each other again.

But she must not let her own feelings for Griffin colour her interpretations of his comments. When he said he had hated every moment she had been away from him, he had surely meant in the role he had undertaken as her guardian.

'Perhaps once Lady Francesca has returned we might all be better informed as to how we might proceed,' Bea spoke again softly.

Griffin clenched his jaw at the mere mention of the other woman. 'It is to be hoped so.' He really did not think that he could leave Bea behind when he departed Latham Manor. Just the thought of it was enough to make him clench his fists in frustration.

And he knew that feeling no longer had anything to do with thoughts of Bea remaining here in the company of Christian, and everything to do with—

'My dears, what a lovely surprise it is to see you all gathered together in my drawing room!' Francesca Latham swept into the room, blond head tilted at a haughty angle, blue eyes aglow with that mocking humour she so often favoured. 'I could barely credit it when Shaw informed me of our exulted company, Latham.' She moved to her husband's side. 'And I see dear Beatrix has also returned to us, in the company of the Duke of Sutherland.' That hard blue gaze now settled on Bea.

Griffin had stood up upon that lady's entrance. 'I am sure that must be as much of a pleasant surprise to you as it was to Sir Walter?'

'But of course.' That hard blue gaze now met his challengingly.

Griffin placed his clenched fists behind his back as he resisted the urge he felt to reach out and shake the truth from this woman.

Now that he was here he knew he could not leave here today until he knew whether this woman was Bea's friend or foe. And to hell with the politeness of manners! He was tired of this tedious social dance. He wished now only for the truth. 'You had perhaps not expected her to be here at all?'

Lady Francesca shrugged her elegant shoulders. 'I am sure Latham is not so strict as to begrudge Beatrix time spent with her new friends.'

Griffin's nostrils flared. 'But you, of all people, must know she was not staying with friends.' No matter what the situation, whether Francesca Latham believed Bea to have eloped or been kidnapped, she almost certainly knew that Bea had not been visiting friends these past weeks.

'Griffin—'

'Rotherham—'

'Is that not so, madam?' Griffin ignored both Christian and Aubrey as they rose to their feet in protest at his blunt methods, his gaze now locked in a silent battle with Francesca Latham.

'I am not sure I care for the way in which you are addressing my wife, Rotherham,' Sir Walter blustered uncomfortably.

Still Griffin's gaze remained locked with that hard and mocking one of Francesca Latham's. 'Your wife, sir, is either a liar or a traitor—and I for one wish to know which it is!'

'Griffin?' Bea looked up at him anxiously as he appeared to have forgotten everything the four of them had spoken of this morning, before she had departed for Latham Manor with Christian Seaton. Indeed, Griffin now appeared so coldly angry, as he and her aunt locked gazes, that it seemed the two of them had forgotten they were even in the company of others.

Implying a past rift much deeper than merely that he did not care for his neighbour's wife.

It appeared so to Bea. And she could think of only one reason why such tension might have arisen between two such handsome people. A past love affair that had not ended well.

The idea of Griffin having been intimately involved with Lady Francesca so sickened Bea that she could raise no further protest regarding the bluntness of his conversation.

'What on earth are you on about, Rotherham?' Sir Walter was red-faced with anger. 'You are either foxed or mad. Either way, you will apologise to my wife forthwith.'

'I will neither apologise nor retract my statement,' Griffin bit out harshly. 'You will answer the accusation, Lady Francesca. And you will do so now.'

'Remember my grandson, Griffin,' Lord Maystone cautioned softly.

'I have not forgotten,' Griffin assured him gruffly. 'As I have not forgotten the manner in which I found Bea, following her abduction and days of being held prisoner.' His voice hardened as he continued to look coldly at Lady Latham.

'Abducted? Held prisoner?' Sir Walter looked totally bewildered. 'But Beatrix has been staying with friends—is that not so, Francesca?'

Throughout the whole of this exchange Francesca Latham had remained strangely silent, a contemptuous smile curving her lips as she continued to meet Griffin's gaze unflinchingly.

'Is that so, Lady Francesca?' Griffin now snapped scathingly.

She remained silent for several more long seconds before she gave a weary sigh as she stepped away from her husband and into the centre of the room. 'Is there any point in my continuing with the farce?' she finally taunted in a bored voice.

Griffin's jaw tightened. 'None whatsoever.'

'Very well.' She gave a disgusted shake of her head as she turned to look at Bea. 'So you have been warming Rotherham's bed for this past week.'

'Do not make this situation any more difficult for yourself than it already is,' Griffin warned through clenched teeth.

Hard blue eyes swept over him mockingly. 'I do not in the least begrudge you the warmth, Rotherham,' she drawled. 'Why should I, when I had your wife warming my own bed for so many months before she died?'

Bea felt the colour leave her cheeks even as she saw Griffin stumble back a step.

His own face became deathly pale as he now stared at Francesca Latham in horror. '*You* are "darling Frank"?'

She bared her teeth in a humourless smile. 'So Felicity liked to refer to me as, yes.'

'The two of you were lovers?'

'For many months.' Francesca Latham nodded with satisfaction.

'Francesca!'

'Oh, do be quiet, Walter,' his wife snapped dismissively as she gave him a contemptuous glance. 'We have not shared a bed for years, and now you know the reason why. I have always preferred my own sex,' she continued conversationally. 'Of course, Felicity did become a tad over-possessive and demanding, forcing me to end our association, but whoever would have thought the little ninny would have drowned herself for love of me? Quite tedious, I do assure you.' She gave an irritated shake of her head.

Bea had not been able to take her eyes off Griffin since her aunt had announced her past intimate relationship with his late wife.

Or to wonder if, as Seaton had implied yesterday, she had been mistaken in believing that the happiness Griffin had known in his marriage was the reason he had never remarried. He might have loved his wife, certainly, but he also seemed to have known that his wife's love had not belonged to him.

'But we digress,' Lady Francesca continued pleasantly. 'I take it the two other gentlemen here also wish to see justice done? As I thought.' She nodded at the silence that greeted her question. 'What happens next? Am I to be dragged away in shackles and tortured until I tell you everything I know?'

Griffin roused himself from the shock of hearing the truth of Felicity's betrayal, of their marriage bed and of him. Of learning that his wife's lover, Frank, had not been a man at all, but a woman. Francesca Latham, in truth.

At the same time as he could not help but feel a certain lightening of his heart at learning it had not been *him* in particular whom Felicity had found so physically repellent. That her sexual preference would have made her feel disgust at the idea of a physical relationship with any man.

That her suicide, by drowning herself in the lake at Stonehurst Park, had not been as a way of escaping him and their marriage, but because the woman she loved had rejected her.

Strange to experience such a sense of euphoria in the midst of such chaos. And yet that was exactly how Griffin now felt. As if a heavy weight of guilt and self-loathing had been lifted from his shoulders.

As if that truth had now freed him to try to win Bea's heart for himself.

Were it not for the existence of Michael, of course.

'Was that not what you did to Bea?' Griffin now accused hardly. 'Are you not the one responsible for beating Bea, with the help of your associate Jacob Harker?'

'What is he talking about, Francesca?' Sir Walter seemed to have deflated into being a shell of himself in the past few minutes, his rosy cheeks now a sickly shade of grey.

'Do not tax your brain about it, Latham,' his wife dismissed mockingly. 'You would be far better to attend to your horses and your hounds.'

Latham attempted to rouse himself. 'You will answer me, madam. Who is this man Harker? What have you done that Rotherham now accuses you of being a traitor? It is something to do with that worthless half brother of yours, is it not?' He puffed angrily. 'I always knew he would be nothing but trouble.'

'Be silent, Latham!' His wife turned on him angrily, cheeks flushed. 'You are not fit to so much as speak my brother's name.'

'Half brother,' Sir Walter rallied defiantly. 'Sir Rupert Colville is only your half brother. A weak, lily-livered anarchist bent on bringing down the Crown.'

'I said be quiet!' Lady Francesca flew at

him, hands raised, fingers bent into talons, her face an ugly mask.

Christian was closest to the couple, managing to grasp Francesca Latham about her waist and pull her back before she could reach her husband with those talons. Once she was in his grasp, he secured her more tightly by pulling her arms down and also holding them captive within his grasp as he stood behind her.

Bea had found herself unable to move or speak as the horror of this scene was played out before her.

The revelations about Griffin's wife and Francesca Latham.

The knowledge that it had in all possibility been Francesca Latham herself who had administered Bea's beatings during her week of captivity. Hence the reason she had never spoken in Bea's presence?

As the events of that weekend she had spent with her aunt at the home of Sir Rupert Colville now came back to her. 'You were completely mistaken in your suspicions towards me at your half brother's home, madam.' She got up to stand in front of Francesca Latham. 'At the time I did not understand any of the conversation I overheard between you and Sir Rupert. How could I, when I did not know then that an eight-year-old boy had been cruelly taken from his parents and was being used as blackmail against his influential grandfather?' She gave a shake of her head before turning to Aubrey Maystone. 'My Lord, I think you will find your grandson is being held prisoner at Sir Rupert Colville's home in Worcestershire.'

'Why, you little—'

'Have a care, madam!' Christian warned through gritted teeth as his prisoner would have made a lunge for Bea. 'You have seriously wronged two gentlemen who are close friends of mine, and you have caused great distress and pain to a lady wholly undeserving of such treatment. As such I will have no compunction in taking steps to silence you if you should give me reason to do so.'

'Do as you wish with me.' Francesca tossed her head unconcernedly. 'You may cut off the head of the snake but two more will grow in my place!'

'I do not believe for one moment that you

are the head of this particular snake,' Griffin scorned. 'Nor your milksop brother, either. Neither of you is intelligent enough,' he added with hard derision. 'And I believe we will leave it to the Crown to decide whether or not to cut off both your heads.'

All the colour now drained from Francesca's cheeks. 'How can you remain loyal to such a man as the Prince Regent? A man who overindulges himself in every way possible, spending money he does not have on things he does not need, and to the detriment of his own people.'

'Oh, please, spare us your warped idea of patriotism!' Maystone dismissed. 'Also be assured, madam, that if my grandson is not returned to me unharmed, then I shall personally recommend the hardest sentence imaginable to the Prince Regent, for your crimes against both him personally and to England,' he added grimly.

Hatred now gleamed in those cold blue eyes. 'My brother should have disposed of the boy when I advised him to.'

'You will be quiet, madam!' Bea was shaking with anger at this woman's added cruelty, when Lord Maystone had already suffered so much during these past weeks of uncertainty as to whether his grandson still lived. 'Your grandson is unharmed, Lord Maystone,' she reassured him gently.

He blinked his uncertainty. 'You are sure?'

She nodded. 'I realise now that I was abducted and beaten because it was he that Lady Francesca and her brother spoke of that day I overheard the two of them talking together. Sir Rupert Colville was adamant that he would care for the boy as if he were his own. At the time I thought he spoke of an orphaned ward or nephew. Having recently been orphaned myself, my heart ached for the little boy. For the loneliness he must feel. I had no idea of the truth of the conversation I had overheard.' She gave a bewildered shake of her head.

'Michael truly is unharmed?' There was such hope in Lord Maystone's voice.

Bea gave a puzzled frown as she heard Griffin draw his breath in sharply before she answered the older man gently. 'I truly believe that Sir Rupert Colville will have ensured

Michael has remained unharmed, yes. Sir Rupert is not a man who enjoys physical violence.'

'Unlike you, madam, who enjoys nothing more than beating those who are more helpless than yourself.' Griffin's eyes glittered with anger as he looked contemptuously down his nose at Francesca. 'Where is Harker now?'

Francesca now seemed less defiant than she had a few moments ago. 'I presume he is in his hovel of a cottage, where I was forced to stay hidden during the week of Beatrix's imprisonment.'

Griffin's eyes widened. 'Harker lives in a cottage on my own estate?'

'His name is not Harker but Harcourt, and he is nephew to your own housekeeper,' Lady Francesca taunted.

Which explained, Griffin realised, why none in the area had reported seeing anyone suspicious or unknown to them. But did that also mean that Mrs Harcourt—?

'The old dragon has no idea of Jacob's political views, if that is what you are now thinking,' the blonde-haired traitor dismissed mockingly. 'Not that any of this matters now.' She took in everyone present in the room with one sweeping glance. 'You may rescue Maystone's grandson, arrest Jacob, Rupert and myself, do with us what you will. But, as I have stated, there are plenty of others who will happily take our place in securing Napoleon's freedom.'

'There are even more of us who will ensure they do not succeed,' Christian assured her grimly.

And no doubt Griffin would have to be one of them, he accepted heavily.

But once Maystone's grandson, Michael, was freed and returned to his family, once the Corsican was safely away from England and secured in exile, *then* he might discharge his duties to the Crown once and for all, and return to his estate in Lancashire.

Return to Bea.

Chapter Fifteen

Ten days later

'His Grace, the Duke of Rotherham, is here to see you, My Lady,' Shaw announced from the doorway of the drawing room in Latham Manor.

Bea's heart leapt in her chest at the news that Griffin was back in Lancashire, and she tensed as she looked up from the book she had been reading, as she sat in the window seat enjoying the last of the day's sunlight. 'You are sure the Duke is here to see me and not Sir Walter?'

Bea had not seen Griffin since Lady Francesca and her associate, Jacob Harcourt, had been placed in custody, and he had set off immediately for Worcestershire with Christian

Seaton and Lord Maystone, their intention to liberate the latter's grandson from the home of Lady Francesca's half brother.

But not before it had been discussed and decided that Bea should remain here with her real guardian, Sir Walter, while the other gentlemen were gone. She would far rather have accompanied them on their rescue mission, but had accepted that she would only have slowed them down, and no doubt have been in the way too.

Plus someone had to remain and offer some comfort to Sir Walter. The poor man was devastated, both by the revelations of his wife's affair with Griffin's wife, and by Lady Francesca's treasonous actions, and her subsequent arrest. Bea felt that she might at least be of some help to him by remaining here.

That had indeed proved to be the case, the two of them spending much time together as Sir Walter adjusted and accepted that his wife now faced many charges, including kidnapping and treason.

But he was a pragmatic man, and, having also learnt of his wife's sexual relations with another woman, seemed to have hardened his heart to her fate. Indeed, he was currently out riding his new hunter, having resumed his normal activities several days ago.

They had received word from Griffin after the rescue of Michael, Lord Maystone's grandson, had been as successful as they had hoped. Sir Rupert Colville was also now in custody, and the other three gentlemen had been on their way to London to reunite the little boy with his parents.

Bea had resigned herself to not seeing Griffin again now that he was returned to London.

'His Grace asked for you specifically, My Lady,' the butler now assured her.

'Then you may show him in, Shaw.' Bea nodded.

She turned to quickly check her appearance in the mirror, her mouth having gone dry at thoughts of seeing Griffin again.

At thoughts of the heartache of the two of them meeting and greeting each other as if they were polite strangers.

When that was the last thing they were.

Or ever could be, as far as Bea was concerned.

Her heart almost jumped completely out of her chest as Griffin strode purposefully into the room, not pausing at the doorway but heading straight over to where Bea still stood near the window.

He looked so dark and handsome in his perfectly tailored black superfine, worn with a grey waistcoat and grey pantaloons, his black Hessians gleaming.

So dearly beloved.

'Your Grace.' Bea affected a curtsy, head bent so that Griffin should not see the tears of happiness glistening in her eyes just at the sight of him.

'Bea?' Griffin gave a dark frown as he reached out to place a hand beneath the softness of her chin and raise her face so that he might better see her expression.

These past ten days had been both very successful and equally frustrating.

Maystone's grandson was reunited with his ecstatic family.

Several more of the conspirators to liberate Bonaparte were also now in custody.

The Corsican was well on his way to his remote place of exile.

The English Crown and its people could breathe easily again, for a time at least.

Griffin had also informed Maystone that he had carried out his last mission for the Crown, and intended to retire to his estate in Lancashire.

All of those things had been positive.

The negative had been Griffin's own enforced separation from Bea. Days and days when he had not so much as been able to set sight on her.

Days when she would no doubt have been left to her own thoughts for hours at a time, and have decided that Griffin Stone, the gruff Duke of Rotherham, had no place in the life she now led in quiet solitude with her guardian.

Griffin's own newfound freedom, from believing that the unhappiness of his marriage had been his fault, and that he was also responsible for Felicity's suicide, now sat light as a bird upon his shoulders. Most of all, he now accepted that he could never have made someone like Felicity happy.

The knowledge that Michael had not been the love of Bea's life after all, but Maystone's grandson, had come as even more welcome news. Michael had become a spectre in Bea's dreams only because of the warmth of her heart, her concern for a little boy she had believed to be orphaned, like herself.

That knowledge was the only thing that had kept Griffin sane as he'd dealt with all the other matters in need of his attention before he was free to return to Lancashire.

To return to Bea.

She looked so very beautiful. She was wearing a gown he had never seen before. No doubt one of her own, which had now been delivered from the house in Worcestershire. A gown of the palest blue silk that made her skin appear both pale and luminescent.

Her face appeared a little thinner than Griffin remembered, but that was surely to be expected after the upset of the previous weeks. And the added knowledge that it was her own aunt who was responsible for her abduction and the beatings she had received while held prisoner in the filthy woodcutters' shed.

One of Griffin's last instructions, before he'd departed Stonehurst Park in the company of Christian and Maystone ten long days ago, had been for that shed to be burnt to the ground. That not a single sliver of wood was to remain.

And now here was Bea, looking more beautiful to him than ever.

But with a new wariness in those deep blue eyes as she looked up at him questioningly.

Griffin did his best to gentle his own expression, when what he really wanted to do was take Bea in his arms and kiss her until they were both senseless. A move guaranteed, he suspected, to increase rather than lessen that look of apprehension!

'Are you well, Bea?' he enquired guardedly.

Bea had managed to blink away her tears, and she now offered Griffin a reassuring smile. 'I am perfectly well, thank you. Sir Walter has proved to be an amiable companion these past ten days.'

Griffin removed his fingers from beneath her chin but still studied her intently. 'You are comfortable here, then?'

She moistened her lips before speaking. 'Sir Walter is my guardian. Where else should I go?'

'You seemed to enjoy living at Stonehurst Park.'

Bea gave him a quick glance before turning away to look out of the window facing out towards the gardens at the side of the house. 'I take it you will not be remaining there for long yourself, now that your other business is resolved?' Indeed, she had no idea why Griffin had come back to Stonehurst at all, when there must be so much to do in London now.

Although she was not disappointed that he had; just to see him again, to be with him, to *smell* that unique smell that was Griffin— a combination of lemon, sandalwood and a healthy man in his prime—was enough to make her pulse beat faster. In fact, she would be surprised if Griffin could not hear the loud beating of her heart caused just by being near him again.

But it would be foolish of her to read any more into his visit to Latham Manor this morning than a courtesy call. To ensure that Bea was happy with her new guardian.

'I have stepped down from my work for the Crown, Bea.'

She was frowning slightly as she turned her head to look over her shoulder at him. 'You are perhaps tired of the intrigue and danger?'

Griffin gave a smile. 'I believe I would describe it more that I have found a reason to live.'

Bea's expression softened. 'I am so sorry for the things you have learnt about your late wife. It must have been such a shock to you.' She gave a shake of her head. 'I cannot imagine—'

'It was a relief, Bea,' he cut in firmly. 'Such a blessed relief,' he breathed thankfully. 'For years now I have blamed myself for the failure of my marriage, for not loving Felicity, or she me, so much so that she had preferred to take her own life rather than suffer to live with me another day. To finally know, even in such a way as I learnt the truth, that I was not responsible has caused me to hope—to dare to hope...'

Bea turned fully to face him, her gaze

searching on his face as it now seemed to her that Griffin looked at her with hope in his expressive grey eyes. 'What is it you hope for, Griffin?' she prompted huskily.

His smile became rueful. 'What every man hopes for, I suspect. To be happy with the woman he loves.'

Bea's heart leapt once again in her chest. 'And do you already have such a woman in your life?'

Griffin drew in a sharp breath, knowing he still had much he needed to say before he went any further with this conversation. 'There are things I should tell you about myself, Bea. Things I have not shared, until very recently, with anyone beyond my closest friends. My father's indifference to me during my childhood being one of them.'

'You must try not to blame your father too much for that, Griffin,' she put in quickly. 'Christian told me a little of that situation,' she explained guiltily as Griffin raised questioning brows. 'He did not mean to break any confidences, he was merely trying to explain—to explain—'

'The reason for some of my gruffness of nature, no doubt,' Griffin guessed dryly.

'I do not find you in the least taciturn, Griffin,' she reproved primly.

'No?'

'You are everything that is amiable as far as I am concerned,' she insisted.

'Thank you,' Griffin murmured huskily. 'But we digress.' He straightened. 'Something else I never talked of was the utter failure of my marriage.' He sighed. 'I realise the reason for that now. I accept it. But for those two reasons I have for years believed myself to be unlovable rather than just unloved.'

'Your friends all love you dearly,' she told him.

'Yes, I believe they do,' he acknowledged softly. 'But I had believed myself too dour, too austere, too physically overbearing, to deserve the love of any decent woman. I have lived my life accordingly, never wanting, never expecting, never *asking* for more than I had.'

The slenderness of Bea's throat moved as she swallowed. 'And that has now changed?'

'Completely,' Griffin stated without hesitation. 'Now I want it all. The wife. The children. The happy home. The love of the woman whom I love in return. My homes filled with vases of flowers,' he added ruefully.

Bea could barely breathe, so great was her own hope now that Griffin was talking to her of these things for a reason. 'And have you come here so that I might wish you well on this venture?'

'I want so much more from you than that, Bea,' he assured her firmly. 'I want, one day, for you to be my wife, the mother of my children, the mistress of my happy home, the woman who might love me as I have loved and continue to love you, and who will fill our homes with vases of flowers. I am more than happy to be patient, of course, to woo you, to court you, as you deserve to be—'

'But—I overheard you tell Seaton that our lovemaking was a mistake.'

'Because I believed you to be in love with the man you called out for in your sleep. A man called Michael.'

'Lord Maystone's grandson?'

'I did not know that at the time, Bea. I believed that by loving you, by making love with you, I was encouraging you to be unfaithful to the man you loved. It was only when May-stone finally referred to his grandson as Michael that I realised the truth.' Griffin was prevented from saying more as Bea launched herself into his arms. 'Bea?' he groaned even as his arms closed tightly about her and he crushed her against his much harder body.

Bea beamed up at him, eyes glowing. 'I find I am not patient at all, Griffin. I want all of those things you described *now*. I want *you* now,' she added shyly.

'Bea?' Griffin still looked down at her uncertainly.

She reached up to curve her hands about the hardness of his cheeks as she smiled up at him. 'I already love you, Griffin,' she told him firmly. 'I believe I have loved you almost since the moment I first opened my eyes and saw you seated beside my bed acting as my protector. And that love has only continued to grow every moment of every day since. I *love* you, Griffin,' she repeated emotionally.

He looked uncertain, confused, two emotions Bea had never associated with this strong and decisive man. 'Are you sure you are not confusing gratitude with love?'

'Of course, I am grateful for your having rescued me, and caring for me even though you had no idea who I was or where I came from; what sort of woman would I be if I were not?' she dismissed indulgently. 'I am grateful for all that, but it is you that I love, Griffin. The man, the lover, not the rescuer. These last few days, of not knowing if I would ever see you again, have passed in a haze of agony for me,' she acknowledged huskily. 'I love you so much, Griffin, I cannot bear to be apart from you, even for a moment.'

It was so much how Griffin felt in regard to Bea. 'Will you marry me, Bea, and be my duchess?'

'I will marry you, and gladly, but so that we need never be separated again, not to become your duchess,' she answered him without hesitation.

Griffin grinned and gave a heartfelt whoop of gladness before he claimed her lips with his own.

* * *

'If you do not mind, I believe the wedding must be soon, my love,' he murmured indulgently some time later, as the two of them sat together upon the sofa, Bea's head resting comfortably on his shoulder, his arms about her as he continued to hold her close. 'I find I want to make love to you again so very much, and I should not like our heir to make his appearance eight, or even seven, months after the wedding.'

Bea chuckled softly, so happy to be with Griffin again, to know that he loved her as much as she loved him, that they would never be parted ever again. 'I believe it should be possible for a Special Licence to be arranged for a man who has been so loyal to the Crown for so many years?'

Griffin chuckled softly. 'I believe you might be right, my love.'

'Sir Walter will give me away and Christian can stand up with you.'

'Christian is not in England at the moment,' he confided.

Bea looked up at him searchingly. 'Is he in danger?' she finally asked with concern.

Griffin felt a momentary twinge of that past jealousy before just as quickly dismissing it; Bea loved him. He had no doubt of it and he never would. 'Not that I am aware, no,' he answered dismissively. 'I am no longer privy to such knowledge, Bea, for Christian's sake, more than my own.'

'Of course you are not.' Bea once again settled herself on his shoulder. 'Then one of your other friends will have to stand up with you, for I find I do not wish to wait either.'

Which was reason enough for Griffin to begin kissing her all over again…

* * * * *

Don't miss the next book in Carole Mortimer's dazzling DANGEROUS DUKES *duet:* CHRISTIAN SEATON: DUKE OF DANGER *coming September 2015!*

MILLS & BOON®

The Rising Stars Collection!

This fabulous four-book collection features 3-in-1 stories from some of our talented writers who are the stars of the future! Feel the temperature rise this summer with our ultra-sexy and powerful heroes. Don't miss this great offer—buy the collection today to get one book free!

**Order yours at
www.millsandboon.co.uk/risingstars**

MILLS & BOON®

&HISTORICAL

AWAKEN THE ROMANCE OF THE PAST

0815/04